How many left?

One man from the first car, at least three from the third, if he'd taken out its driver. Bolan still had work to do, and he was running out of time before some passing driver heard the sounds of battle and called the cops.

The one thing Bolan would not do, regardless of the circumstances, was initiate a firefight with police. He'd made a vow that he would never drop the hammer on a cop. Law enforcement officers, in Bolan's mind, were "soldiers of the same side." He'd evade them by any means, but would always stop short of lethal force.

Which meant he had to mop up his remaining enemies and get out of there before the police arrived.

Tick-tock.

He was about to go after the shooters from the third car when a flash of light alerted him to trouble. It was the Marauder's dome light, coming on because one of its doors had opened. The woman bolting out of panic at the gunfire? Or had someone found her?

Either way, he had to check it out, but he couldn't leave enemies behind while his back was turned.

Mouthing a curse, the Executioner moved out.

MACK BOLAN ®
The Executioner

THE EXECUTIONER®
DON PENDLETON'S

BLOOD RITES

YUMA COUNTY LIBRARY DIST.

A GOLD EAGLE BOOK FROM
W✪RLDWIDE®

TORONTO • NEW YORK • LONDON
AMSTERDAM • PARIS • SYDNEY • HAMBURG
STOCKHOLM • ATHENS • TOKYO • MILAN
MADRID • WARSAW • BUDAPEST • AUCKLAND

If you purchased this book without a cover you should be aware
that this book is stolen property. It was reported as "unsold and
destroyed" to the publisher, and neither the author nor the
publisher has received any payment for this "stripped book."

For Master-at-Arms Second Class Michael Anthony Monsoor
(April 5, 1981–September 29, 2006)

First edition June 2015

ISBN-13: 978-0-373-64439-1

Special thanks and acknowledgment to
Mike Newton for his contribution to this work.

Blood Rites

Recycling programs
for this product may
not exist in your area.

Copyright © 2015 by Worldwide Library

All rights reserved. Except for use in any review, the
reproduction or utilization of this work in whole or in part
in any form by any electronic, mechanical or other means,
now known or hereinafter invented, including xerography,
photocopying and recording, or in any information storage
or retrieval system, is forbidden without the written permission
of the publisher, Worldwide Library, 225 Duncan Mill Road,
Don Mills, Ontario M3B 3K9, Canada.

This is a work of fiction. Names, characters, places and incidents are
either the product of the author's imagination or are used fictitiously,
and any resemblance to actual persons, living or dead, business
establishments, events or locales is entirely coincidental.

® and TM are trademarks of the publisher. Trademarks indicated
with ® are registered in the United States Patent and Trademark
Office, the Canadian Intellectual Property Office and in other
countries.

Printed in U.S.A.

Destroy the seed of evil, or it will grow up to your ruin.
—Aesop,
"The Swallow and Other Birds"

Evil takes root wherever good men close their eyes. Only scorched earth can kill the seeds.
—Mack Bolan

THE
MACK BOLAN
LEGEND

Nothing less than a war could have fashioned the destiny of the man called Mack Bolan. Bolan earned the Executioner title in the jungle hell of Vietnam.

But this soldier also wore another name—Sergeant Mercy. He was so tagged because of the compassion he showed to wounded comrades-in-arms and Vietnamese civilians.

Mack Bolan's second tour of duty ended prematurely when he was given emergency leave to return home and bury his family, victims of the Mob. Then he declared a one-man war against the Mafia.

He confronted the Families head-on from coast to coast, and soon a hope of victory began to appear. But Bolan had broken society's every rule. That same society started gunning for this elusive warrior—to no avail.

So Bolan was offered amnesty to work within the system against terrorism. This time, as an employee of Uncle Sam, Bolan became Colonel John Phoenix. With a command center at Stony Man Farm in Virginia, he and his new allies—Able Team and Phoenix Force—waged relentless war on a new adversary: the KGB.

But when his one true love, April Rose, died at the hands of the Soviet terror machine, Bolan severed all ties with Establishment authority.

Now, after a lengthy lone-wolf struggle and much soul-searching, the Executioner has agreed to enter an "arm's-length" alliance with his government once more, reserving the right to pursue personal missions in his Everlasting War.

Prologue

Dolphin Mall,
Sweetwater, Florida

"He's late," René Bertin announced.

"I *know* he's late," François Raimonde replied. "You think I can't tell time?"

"Just sayin'."

"Well, *stop* sayin', unless you got a way to hurry him."

"How am I supposed to do that?"

"Then shut up."

Raimonde had always wondered why the county named its largest shopping mall after a fish, until somebody told him it was named after a football team. That pacified him for a while, until he learned the team had no connection to the mall, which irritated him again.

Screw it.

The only thing he cared about right now was meeting Roger Dessalines and picking up the bag he was supposed to deliver, with twelve kilos of pure cocaine inside. Dessalines *was* running late, some twenty minutes now, and that was cause for worry, but Raimonde was trying not to let it make him crazy. Bad things happened when he tipped over the edge, as anyone who knew him could attest.

At least, the ones who were still alive.

Bertin muttered something under his breath, and Raimonde felt his cheeks heating up. "What was that?"

"I said why don't he call, if he's gonna be late?"

"You can ask him, if he ever shows up."

"Man, we've been sitting here forever. It ain't good, you know?"

Raimonde knew. Deals like this one were meant to go swiftly and smoothly, no waiting around. Every minute they spent in the mall's parking lot, baking under the sun in their Lexus, raised their level of risk. Mall security circled the property every half hour or so, and they might call police if they figured Raimonde and Bertin looked suspicious. Police meant questions and possibly a search that would reveal their weapons and the gym bag filled with cash.

Bad news, but that wasn't the worst.

They were in posse territory. In Raimonde's opinion this was a stupid place for a handoff, but he hadn't been consulted. Never was, in fact. Just got his orders and obeyed them like a soldier should. But sitting still for any length of time in posse territory was an invitation to disaster.

"Where is he?" Bertin grumbled, not quite whining.

"I told you—"

"Shit! Look there! You see 'em?"

Raimonde followed Bertin's pointing finger and went cold inside, despite the midday heat. A jet-black Lincoln MKT was cruising through the lot, its large grille flashing sunlight like a monster's toothy smile. The blacked-out windows hid most of its passengers, but Raimonde saw the driver and his shotgun rider plain enough, both of them sporting dreads, the wheelman wearing a crocheted Rasta cap.

"What are we gonna do?" Bertin demanded.

"Do our job," Raimonde informed him, reaching underneath his seat for the machine pistol hidden there. Bertin grunted and reached under his baggy jacket to draw a Glock 18 selective-fire model, digging in a pocket to produce a 33-round magazine and swap it for the pistol's normal clip.

"They see us, we're in shit," Bertin declared.

"More likely if we move."

"This is Roger's fault."

"The boss said wait," Raimonde said. "We wait."

And so, they did.

"CHECK OUT THE LEXUS," Shabba Maxwell said.

"Where?" Tyson Eccles asked from the driver's seat.

"Open your eyes."

Neville Bucknor chimed in, from the backseat. "I know that bastard at the wheel."

Eccles eyed the Lexus as they passed it, thirty yards away and rolling slowly in the Dolphin Mall's fire lane. They were Haitians, he was almost sure, even without the word from Bucknor.

"What are we gonna do?" Desmond Salkey asked.

"Same thing we always do," Maxwell said. "They've got no business on our turf."

"You gonna ask the boss?" Eccles said.

"Ask him what?" Maxwell demanded. "He said deal with any bad boys we find comin' up in here."

"Should shoot 'em dead," Salkey chipped in.

"You wanna ask someone," Maxwell said, "give me the wheel and split."

"Ease up, man," Eccles said. "I'm with you, brother."

"No more talking, then. Get out your pieces."

Maxwell's weapon was a Micro-Uzi SMG. His two men in the backseat carried AK-105 Kalashnikov carbines, and Eccles had a twelve-gauge Ithaca 37 Stakeout model shotgun tucked into the map pocket of his driver's door, ready to go.

"Okay," Maxwell told them. "Do this thing!"

"ALL UNITS, CODE 30! We have shots fired at the Dolphin Mall, multiple injuries reported, still in progress."

"Acknowledge that," Corporal Tyrus Jackson told his partner. He was driving their patrol car, letting rookie Rick Lopez handle the radio.

Lopez snatched up the microphone and answered, "Unit 31 responding. We're two minutes out."

Jackson already had the Ford Crown Victoria Police Interceptor up to sixty-five, rolling toward Northwest 117th Avenue. He'd make a right turn there, if no one slammed into their cruiser, and they'd arrive at the mall shortly.

"The Dolphin's massive," he reminded Lopez. "Call back and find out where the shooting is. With multiples, we got no time to waste."

"Roger that."

Lopez raised the dispatcher, and the answer came back with a wisp of static. "Southwest parking lot."

"Ninety seconds, if we're lucky," Lopez said, and cut the link.

Multiple casualties meant a psycho on a rampage, or some kind of gang activity. Jackson was betting on the gangs, but you could never tell. Miami wasn't just a melting pot, it was a *boiling* pot, where races and religions clashed, the rich flaunted their money and the poor wanted a piece of it. In any given year, Miami Metro saw it all, from slaughters in the family to drug burns, hate crimes, even human sacrifice.

But multiples, with a shooting still in progress, meant his day had gone to shit, barely an hour after roll call.

"Here we go," he said, and swung onto the ring road that encircled Dolphin Mall. He heard the gunfire now. Snap, crackle, pop, telling him there were automatic weapons in the mix. Not one, but several, which meant this wasn't just a random head case run amok.

"What do we do?" Lopez asked, sounding worried.

"Same as always," Jackson answered. "Whatever we can."

"BABYLON IS COMIN'," Salkey said, pointing at the police car entering the parking lot.

"I'm not deaf," Maxwell reminded him, reloading as he moved to head off the patrol car.

They'd pinned the Haitians down but hadn't killed them yet, though Maxwell reckoned one was wounded. He'd seen crimson spatters when they started firing on the Lexus, but their targets both returned fire, peppering the Lincoln MKT before Eccles had swung around behind a bulky pickup truck. They'd have to strip and burn the ride when they were finished here, which pissed him off to no end.

And now, police.

Tracking their progress through the parking lot was easy. The siren was wailing, blue and white lights flashing on the roof rack. As they turned into the nearest lane and started toward the Lexus, Maxwell rose before the cruiser, hosing it with Parabellum slugs.

"Die, Babylon!" he shouted as their windshield imploded, the driver's face turning red-raw in an instant. The cruiser swerved and crashed into a station wagon, then stalled.

The young Latino passenger bailed out, whipping a sidearm from its holster, but he wasn't fast enough. Maxwell cut loose on him, the Micro-Uzi's bullets ripping through his brown uniform, releasing scarlet blooms on impact.

"Shoulda worn your vest," he jeered, and turned back to the battle going on behind him.

Two pigs down, two Haitians still to go. Then they'd

torch the Lincoln and find a way back to the boss, to report.

"Party time," Maxwell muttered, and moved off to meet his enemies.

1

Norland, Miami Gardens, Florida

Mack Bolan hit the ground running in Miami. He had driven down from Stony Man Farm, in Virginia, breaking up the journey with an overnight stop in Savannah, Georgia. The drive let him carry the gear he'd picked out for this mission without any hassles from airport security, and if something happened to the car—a confiscated narco-smuggler's Mercury Marauder, whose records had been lost somewhere between its forfeiture and its delivery to Stony Man—there would be no comebacks on Bolan or the Farm.

The warring parties were a tough Jamaican outfit called the Viper Posse, and a Haitian gang whose leaders hadn't bothered thinking up a catchy name. Both dealt in drugs, illegal weapons, human trafficking and sundry lesser rackets. They'd been stepping on each other's toes around Miami for the past two years, the body count increasing, but this last flamboyant battle at the crowded Dolphin Mall caused a ripple out of Washington, propelling Bolan to the Sunshine State.

Nine dead and thirteen wounded in the latest firefight, which was probably a record, even for South Florida. The body count included three known Viper Posse members, two illegal Haitian immigrants, two Miami-Dade police officers, and two shoppers caught in the crossfire. The wounded were bystanders, more cops and a couple of mall security officers. Local law and the feds were all over it, turning Miami's Haitian and Jamaican enclaves upside-down, but cries of racial profiling had touched off protests in the streets, and when you got down to it, no police force in the States could chase the Viper Posse's leaders once they split for home.

That was where Bolan came in.

He didn't need warrants, indictments, subpoenas, or writs of extradition. He wasn't logging evidence for use in court, and didn't have to read a perp his rights before he brought the hammer down. He'd been hunting human predators of one kind or another from his youth until his staged death in Manhattan some years back, with nothing changed except his face and name.

His war was still the same. The opposition's ranks were inexhaustible.

Most of the residents of Kendall, southwest of Coral Gables, were law-abiding people. However, those who stood outside the law had earned a reputation for ferocious violence.

While most posse members were nominal Rastafarians, purportedly worshiping late Ethiopian emperor Haile Selassie I as a god and smoking ganja as a sacrament, the island-spawned gang also swam in a current of Obeah, a West Indian belief system with African roots, akin to Voodoo or Santeria. The practice of Obeah involved blood sacrifice. Animals were ostensibly preferred, but some practitioners were rumored to spill human blood for important rituals, or when they sent a special message to their enemies.

Murder was all the same to Bolan, whether carried out with automatic weapons or machetes, and he normally repaid the predators in kind. He had no fear of "magick," black or white, but recognized that many people felt its draw and thereby left themselves open to victimization.

When superstition crossed the line into mayhem and became a tool for terrorists, the Executioner was ready to step in and shut the circus down.

Beginning now.

GARCELLE BROUARD KNEW she was staring in the face of death as Winston Channer stood before her, showing a ghastly smile. A fall of dusty-looking dreadlocks framed his oval face, eyebrows replaced by rows of small, deliberately inflicted scars, more of them on his cheeks in tight spiral designs. His teeth were either capped or filed to points, so that his smile displayed a double row of fangs.

"You're as good as dead," he told her.

Garcelle kept her face impassive and replied, "So, get it over with."

"Not so fast, child. I've got a message for your family."

"You think that will change the way they deal with you?" She laughed, enjoying the expression on his feral face. "You'll only make things worse."

"Be worse for you, no doubt. Think Daddy will like it if I send ya back in pieces?" Channer narrowed his eyes and asked, "Why are you smiling?"

She kept the mocking smile in place while answering his question. "I'm imagining the things he'll do to you. How long he'll keep you tied up on his table, screaming."

"You like the screams, eh? When I start on you, scream plenty for me, will ya? No one's coming to help you."

That was true, she realized. The Viper Posse occupied this whole apartment complex. She sat in unit 227, bound to a straight-backed wooden chair with plastic zip ties. She could scream until her lungs bled, and the other yardies wouldn't interfere with Channer's fun. Nor would the neighbors, who'd been terrorized into submission when the Viper Posse routed tenants from the Palm Glades complex and converted it into their headquarters.

Police? Forget about them. They patrolled Kendall's white neighborhoods routinely, but required an urgent call to trespass on Jamaican turf around Three Lakes. The last time they'd visited Palm Glades, it sparked a confrontation that sent nine yardies to jail, and seven coppers to the hospital. The gang was not evicted, though, because it kept a battery of top-end lawyers on retainer and possessed a bill of sale for the suburban property.

No. She was on her own, and that was bad.

Fatally bad.

She couldn't bargain with the Viper Posse's local honcho, couldn't bribe her way out of the trap. Channer was bent on capturing her father's territory, taking everything he had, and would not settle for a consolation prize.

She was a pawn to him—or worse, a living sacrifice.

"I don't want to cut your head off first," Channer said. "That spoils my game and tells your daddy he's got nothing left to hope for. Mebbe I should start down on the other end, eh?"

Garcelle tried to imagine what it would feel like, having her feet cut off. Would she bleed out? Not likely, if her captors wanted her alive and suffering. A propane torch would cauterize the wounds, but searing would not stop infection. Not that it would help. Channer would no doubt dismember her completely, long before gangrene could end her misery.

Tell them no more than you have to, she thought grimly. Everybody breaks, but hold on as long as you can. Make the bastards work for it.

"Ten toes it is," Channer declared, and moved off toward the doorway. He opened it and called to someone on the Other Side, "Gimme the little saw, brother. And one of those blue tarps."

BOLAN HAD GONE all out, picking his tools for the Miami mission. Riding with him on the southbound highway was a Steyr AUG assault rifle, a Benelli M4 Super 90 semiautomatic shotgun, a Desert Eagle .44 Magnum pistol, and his favorite Beretta 93R selective-fire side-arm. For long-range work, he'd picked a Barrett M98B sniper rifle. The Barrett is a bolt-action weapon, feeding .338 Lapua Magnum rounds from a ten-round detachable box magazine. Top off that ensemble with spare magazines all around, plus two dozen M68 fragmentation grenades, and the Executioner was ready to rumble.

His first target was a so-called social club, the Kingston House, located on Southwest 80th Street near Snapper Creek Park. Intel from Stony Man identified it as a hangout for the Viper Posse's goons and part-time headquarters for Winston Channer, honcho of the posse in South Florida. Bolan could not predict if Channer would be in when he came calling, but he pegged the odds at fifty-fifty. Either way, demolishing the joint and taking out the posse soldiers he found on-site would send a message to the man in charge, and ultimately back home to Jamaica.

Bolan parked his Mercury a half block north of Kingston House, secured it and set the ear-splitting alarm. If all went well, he wouldn't be gone long, and he'd return to find his rolling arsenal where he had left it. Otherwise, he'd have to improvise.

Leaving his ride, he took the Steyr AUG with an AAC M4-2000 suppressor attached, both handguns and a couple of grenades. It was supposed to be a hit-and-git, not a protracted battle, but he prepped for any snags he could imagine, and a few that didn't come to mind immediately. Bolan's protracted war had taught him that preparedness counted for more than luck.

The place looked dead as he approached it. Never meant to draw outsiders, the exterior was relatively drab: two stories, with beige stucco on the outside, a flat roof, no neon flashing in the night. Unless you were a Viper

Posse member or associate, you had no reason to stop at Kingston House, and any trespassers would be discouraged in a most emphatic way.

He scouted the approach and found no guards watching the street. Given the state of modern CCTV cameras, lookouts might well be watching him from inside, but Bolan wasn't bothered by that possibility. He was expecting opposition.

Counting on it.

He walked behind the club, bringing the Steyr out from underneath his lightweight raincoat. It had drizzled off and on all day, reason enough to wear the coat that hid his hardware, but the time had come to let it rip.

Bolan tried the back door, found it locked and fired a muffled 3-round burst into its dead bolt, shattering the lock. He followed through without a second's hesitation and found himself inside a corridor that passed a kitchen on the left and restrooms on the right. Apparently no one was using either of the two facilities just now. Ahead of him, Bolan heard voices coming from some kind of rec room, half a dozen by the sound of it, engaged in a friendly argument. Above his head, the sound of footsteps told him there were other posse members on the second floor. There was a heady scent of ganja in the air.

"That girl's hot," one of the possemen was saying, "know what I mean?"

"You're speaking true," another said.

"I wouldn't lie to ya," the first voice said.

Bolan crashed the party, counting seven heads around a pool table. He was quiet till one of them spotted him and squawked a warning to the others. Then he began to take them down with nearly silent 5.56 mm NATO rounds. They scrambled, seeking cover, groping for their weapons.

First to draw his pistol was a porky soldier with a rainbow-colored Rasta cap atop his head. Before he had a chance to aim, Bolan's next burst sheared off the left side of his face, but the soldier still managed one wild shot as he was falling, wasted on the ceiling. A shout up there told Bolan that the club's other inhabitants were on alert and pounding toward the stairs.

"WHAT'S THAT?" WINSTON CHANNER demanded, standing over his captive with a hacksaw in his hand.

"Sounds like your boys are shooting each other," Garcelle Brouard told him, smiling.

Channer swung his free hand, striking her across the right cheek. Spitting blood, Garcelle supposed she was fortunate he hadn't used the saw.

"Big man," she sneered, with crimson lips. "Untie me, and we'll see how tough you are."

"I'm gonna fix this, then come back and fix you, hear me?"

"Big talk," she spat at him, expecting to be struck again, but Channer turned away, setting the hacksaw on a nearby table as he left the room. A moment later, he was back again, drawing a switchblade from his pocket, snapping it open as he moved behind her chair.

"Looks like your daddy sent his man to fetch you home. I've got a big surprise for him. He's as good as dead."

She felt the blade pass through the plastic ties that held her arms behind the chair. Then the knife was at her throat, the point drawing a bead of blood below her jawline on the right. Channer's free hand gripped her hair as she slowly rose to stand beside him, measuring her chances of escape.

Not good.

"You think I'm gonna let you go? Not gonna happen, trust me. I want your daddy's man to see your head come off."

Hearing that, she almost turned to grapple with him,

then decided she might have a better chance once they were on the staircase leading to the ground floor. He would be off balance then, distracted by the chaos going on below, and if she timed her move exactly right—

Big if, she thought.

One slip, and he would punch the blade up through her soft palate, into her brain, or simply slash her throat. There'd be no time to cut her head off with the relatively small knife, but Channer didn't need to. He could kill her with a short flick of his wrist, and have the same effect on her father.

Not that it would save Channer.

Garcelle hoped she'd live long enough to see her father's men blast Channer into hamburger and leave him leaking on the stairs. It would be worth it, to die knowing she had outlived the worthless Rasta piece of crap.

He shoved her through the office door, onto the landing and toward the staircase. More shots echoed from below, but they were dying out now. Which side would emerge victorious? She guessed it didn't matter, but she hoped to see Channer's thugs laid out, dead or dying, when they reached the stairs.

Not justice, necessarily, but vengeance.

Other Viper Posse soldiers had collected on the second-story landing, staying well behind their captain and his human shield. They seemed content to let Channer press forward, face the danger on his own and possibly distract the enemy before they joined the fight.

Cowards. Given the chance, she would have spit on them. But there would be no chance. Garcelle knew she was almost out of time, about to die at twenty-six years old.

They reached the stairs and Channer shouted, "Hold on down there! I wanna show you somethin'."

"Come down, then," somebody answered. Not a voice she recognized.

A white man stepped into view, surprising Garcelle. She didn't recognize him, knew she would have remembered that grimly handsome face if they had ever met. Who was he, then? And why was he here, killing Channer's men?

"Who are you?" Channer demanded, tightening his grip on Garcelle's hair, pressing his blade's tip deeper into yielding flesh until she nearly sobbed.

"Is that your last question?" the white man asked.

"How about I cut this gal's head off. How'd that be?"

"You could do that," the gunman said. "But what comes next, without your shield?"

"I'm not joking," Channer snarled. "Ya think I'm scared? I'm going to—"

Before he could complete the thought, the white man raised his weapon, aimed, and fired a shot that seemed to be directed at Garcelle.

THE BULLET FOUND its mark, ripping through Channer's left arm, which was raised to let him clutch the woman's hair. Its impact drove him backward and broke his contact with the hostage, who immediately lurched away from him and tumbled headlong down the stairs. A fall like that could kill you, but she landed at the bottom more or less intact and started struggling to her feet.

"Come on!" he snapped at her, still covering the balcony above. Channer had fallen back, beyond Bolan's line of sight, but others were crowding after him, their faces peeping cautiously downstairs.

Bolan discouraged them with a short burst that ripped through ceiling tiles and brought fragments raining down. A couple gunmen fired blindly in his direction, pistol shots, and missed by yards. Bolan stood his ground and let the woman scramble toward him, fresh blood weeping from her nose and from a cut beneath her jaw.

"Please, get me out of here!" she begged him. "I can pay you!"

"That way," Bolan said, nodding toward the hallway leading to the back door, "while I cover you."

She ran, seeming no worse for having fallen down the stairs. If she was hurt, she managed to disguise it well. Bolan retreated from the staircase, walking backward as he followed her, still covering the Viper Posse shooters on the second floor. Each time one showed his head, Bolan squeezed off a round or two and sent them ducking out of sight.

He heard the back door open as the lady shoved against it, bursting out into the night. She might run off without him, and if so, he wished her well. The last thing Bolan needed was a sidekick looking for sanctuary.

But she didn't run. He found her waiting in the alley, looking frantic. "Don't tell me you *walked* here," she implored, her accent something from the French Caribbean. Haitian, maybe, though there were other possibilities.

If she *was* Haitian, it put her presence at the Kingston House into a new perspective. Not merely a captive, but perhaps a prisoner of war.

"The car's down that way," Bolan told her, pointing. "Half a block."

"You'll take me out of here?"

"I didn't plan to hang around."

"Please hurry, then, before they catch us!"

She was off and running after that, with no idea what Bolan's ride might look like. To delay pursuit, he fired another short burst through the open door, no targets yet in sight, then followed her at double time.

"The Mercury," he told her as he caught up.

"This? It's *old*."

"It's vintage," he corrected, and unlocked the doors remotely, sliding in behind the wheel while she sat next to him.

Downrange, he saw armed men erupting from the back door of their social club, scanning the alley and the street beyond for targets. Bolan left his headlights off as he revved the Marauder's engine, cranking through a tight U-turn, but they were sure to spot him anyway. Less than a minute later, he had two cars in pursuit and gave up the deception, switching on his lights.

"They'll catch us," she worried aloud. "We can't outrun them in this...this...."

"Don't underestimate three hundred ninety cubic inches," Bolan said, still not entirely sure he wanted to escape from Channer's men. More damage could be done by getting rid of them for good, but he required an open killing ground for that, without civilians in his line of fire.

Someplace like the nearby park, perhaps, where he could find some combat stretch, with all the kiddies safely home for dinner, schoolwork and TV time with families.

"They're coming!" his passenger warned.

"Stay down after we stop," he told her.

"Stop! What do—"

"Hang on! We're almost there."

2

The winding road led Bolan through Snapper Creek Park to a deserted visitor's center. A couple of dim lights still burned inside for security's sake. The extra cover wouldn't hurt when he went EVA, and he was hoping the trees around the building would conceal muzzle-flashes from drivers passing by. As for the racket, he could muffle only his own guns. The rest were out of his control until he silenced them by force.

He reached the smallish parking lot and put the Mercury Marauder through a tight bootlegger's turn. Bolan switched off the headlights as he killed the rumbling engine, grabbed the Steyr and was out of there in seconds flat.

"What about me?" his passenger called after him.

"Stay there!" he snapped, and left her, merging with the night.

It wasn't dark for long. Two chase cars were approaching on the same road he had followed. They claimed both lanes, so no one could slip past them, high beams swallowing the darkness, but they weren't in any hurry now. Still making decent time, but nothing risky as they came on, sniffing for an ambush.

To the north, where Bolan could have fled the park along another looping road, a third car was approaching, headlights off, a subtle touch defeated by the widely spaced floodlights. It had been a smart move, sending in another team to cut off his retreat, but Bolan wasn't worried yet.

Three cars, say four men to a ride unless they packed them in like cocktail sausages. A dozen wasn't all that many if he handled it correctly. If he blew it, on the other hand, one man was all it took to bring him down.

Bolan tracked the two cars on his right through the Steyr's integral telescopic sight. He put his first round through the tinted windshield of the chase car rolling down the left-hand lane, approximately where the driver's face should be. The car lurched, started drifting toward a grassy verge, then straightened out and stopped as someone got the steering wheel under control.

By then, Bolan had shifted to the second car and fired another muffled shot, hoping the silencer that doubled as a flash-hider would cover his position. Round two pierced the second windshield with a *plink*, but this car didn't swerve or stall. Instead, it suddenly accelerated toward the parking lot where Bolan's Mercury sat waiting. The chase car's headlights were switching off, three doors already opening before it came to rest.

Call that a miss, on driver number two.

Three men had tumbled from the first car he'd fired on, and he saw four scrambling from the second now. He had a choice to make, and he made it swiftly, spinning toward the third car, still approaching with its lights turned off. He used the glint of floodlights on the windshield as his guide, firing another single shot intended for the driver.

And scored this time, if the reaction of the vehicle was any indication. It stopped short, as if a dead weight had slipped down and landed on the brake pedal, the engine muttering to be unleashed, but for the moment stuck exactly where it sat.

Call that two out of three.

As men erupted from the third car, Bolan swung back

toward the other two. He couldn't trust the night to cover him forever, even with the AUG's suppressor masking his location, but he still had time to do some damage now, before he had to move.

The soldiers sent to kill him were the same sort he'd encountered back at Kingston House, with dreads and baggy shirts intended to evoke an Afro-Caribbean vibe. Their scruffy clothing was in sharp contrast to the bright, shiny weapons they carried, all ready to rip at the first glimpse of a target.

Coming at them any second now.

THE FIRST SHOT SEEMED to come from nowhere. It cracked the windshield and ripped open Lenny Garvey's face. The driver gave a little grunt, as if surprised, then slumped over the steering wheel, taking the vehicle off course till Gordon Crawford reached across and disentangled Lenny, gave the wheel a twist and thrust a leg between the driver's dead ones, stamping on the brake.

"Get out of the car!" he shouted at the backseat soldiers, leading by example as he bailed out and hit the pavement on one shoulder, gasping at the sudden pain. "Damn it!"

Crawford kept moving, damn the pain. He hadn't heard the shot, although his window was open, and had seen no muzzle-flash. Same story when the second chase car took a hit, but this one evidently missed the driver, since he charged on toward a parking lot some fifty yards ahead of them, and then squealed to a halt.

The plug car, coming at them from the north, took the next hit. Crawford was up and running when it swerved and stalled. He still had no sight of the enemy, but knew the white man wasn't firing from the car he'd abandoned in the parking lot.

Two targets, neither of them visible as yet, and Crawford couldn't go back to his boss if either one eluded him.

Channer was hurt and raging, gone to ground by now, away from what was left of Kingston House before the pigs from Babylon rolled in.

Crawford clutched an M4 carbine loaded with a Sure-Fire 60-round magazine, two more stuffed into pockets in his floppy shapeless jacket, worn with sleeves rolled back over his tattooed forearms. In his belt was wedged a Beretta 92G-SD pistol, and he worried that it might pop loose while he was running.

Crawford dropped behind a tree whose trunk was stout enough to cover him from any shooters working near the building. One armed man should be his only adversary, but he couldn't sell the woman short, either. She had an instinct for survival, and you never knew who might be handy with a weapon, if one fell into their hands.

Armed or not, she had to die.

The notion of a white man bursting in to save her boggled Crawford's mind, but he couldn't afford to focus on that now. Survival was his one priority—which meant getting through the firefight with his skin intact and finishing the job he'd been sent to do. If he fell short, the death awaiting him at Winston Channer's hands would make a gunshot seem like Heaven's blessing.

He looked around and found the other two survivors from his car still crouching near it, angling weapons toward the visitor's center, waiting for a target to reveal itself. Beyond them, four men from the second car were circling through the shadows cast by the building, seeking the man who'd brought them under fire.

Crawford hissed at his two lazy soldiers, then took a chance and raised his voice when they ignored him. "Move your ass!" he commanded, punctuating the order with an emphatic motion from his rifle.

Glowering, the two of them broke cover—and a bullet instantly found Byron Taylor, spinning him around with blood spraying as he hit the road facedown. Ini Munroe, beside him, gave a yelp and sprinted toward the building where the other soldiers were engaged in tracking down the sniper.

"You bring his head to me!" Crawford shouted after them. "And find the woman!"

Munroe offered no acknowledgment, but kept on running with his head tucked low, ready to open fire with his Kalashnikov if threatened. Trouble was, the threat might not be recognized until another bullet struck and laid him out.

Crawford knew he'd have to move soon. Hiding while his soldiers did the dirty work might be the normal mode of operation in some syndicates, but in the Viper Posse, leadership was understood to mean precisely that. Word got around if someone in the upper ranks was slacking.

Which was the first step toward a bloody end.

Cursing, he edged around the tree, taking a precious moment to prepare himself, then burst from cover, shouting, "Burn in hell!"

Whatever waited on the Other Side, two of his men had solved the mystery already, and instinct told him they would soon have company.

BOLAN SAW THE second runner drop, then swung back toward the quartet from the second chase car. They were fanning out along the east wall of the visitor's center, crouching as they scuttled through the shadows, searching for the shooter who had slain their comrades. So far, none of them had spotted Bolan, but his good luck couldn't last much longer as they closed the gap, advancing steadily.

One way to keep from showing muzzle-flashes was to lob a frag grenade.

He palmed one of the M68s, pulled its pin and pitched the grenade overhand. The bomb had a three-second fuse plus an impact fuse for backup, which would blow the charge three to seven seconds after it hit the ground or some solid object. No backup was needed this time, though, as the timer worked efficiently to fill the night with smoke, fire, shrapnel and screams.

It wasn't a clean sweep, of course. The shooters had been smart enough to spread out while they hunted, so that one burst from an automatic weapon couldn't drop them all at once. Two took the brunt of it, riddled with jagged shards of steel, and one shooter's arm separated from his trunk and went airborne, hand still clutching his machine pistol. The little stutter gun erupted when it hit the pavement, emptying its magazine with one long burst.

The two remaining soldiers from the second car were stunned, one of them limping as he tried to turn and flee, but neither one of them was going anywhere. Bolan had spotted them while the shrapnel flew, and clipped the limper with a single round between the shoulder blades that punched out through his chest and sprayed the nearby stucco wall with blood. It took a moment for the dead man's injured legs to get the message, then they folded, dropping him facedown onto the sidewalk.

That left one, and he was running for his life, firing backward, blindly, with some kind of stubby Kalashnikov carbine. Bolan recognized the Russian weapon's sound and ducked a stream of slugs that fanned the air above his head, finding his spot by pure dumb luck.

The Executioner framed the shooter with the Steyr's sight and hit him with a double-tap that ripped into his left side, low, an inch or two above his waistline. Nearly lifted off his feet, the soldier spun, dreadlocks fanned out around his screaming face like serpents on Medusa's scalp, and went down firing, landing heavily, his back against the wall.

It shouldn't take him long to bleed out, but he was a

danger in the meantime, his Kalashnikov still spitting death in Bolan's general direction. One more shot from twenty yards drilled through his forehead, bounced his head against the stucco as it emptied through a fist-size exit wound, then let him slump, slack-limbed, into the awkward sprawl of death.

How many left?

He made it one man from the first car, at least three from the third, if he'd taken out its driver. Bolan still had work to do, and he was running out of time before some passing driver heard the sounds of battle coming from the park and called the cops.

The one thing Bolan would not do, regardless of the circumstances, was initiate a firefight with Miami-Dade Police. He'd made a vow, at the beginning of his lonely war, that he would never drop the hammer on a cop. Law enforcement officers, in Bolan's mind, were "soldiers of the same side." He'd evade them by whatever means he could, but always stopping short of lethal force.

Which meant he had to mop up his remaining enemies and haul ass out of there before the police arrived.

Tick-tock.

He was about to go after the shooters from the third car when a flash of light from Bolan's right alerted him to trouble. It was the Marauder's dome light, coming on because one of its doors had opened. The woman bolting out of panic at the gunfire? Or had someone found her?

Either way, he had to check it out, but he couldn't leave enemies behind while his back was turned.

Mouthing a curse, the Executioner moved out.

GARCELLE BROUARD HAD heard enough, huddled against the floorboards of the white man's car, to know that he was never coming back. She should have bolted instantly, the moment she was left alone, but something—maybe con-

fidence in how he'd handled Channer and his soldiers at
the Kingston House—had made her play along.

And now, was it too late?

She had to find out for herself.

She fumbled blindly for the door latch, reaching up, behind her head, afraid to show herself with bullets flying
all around. She nearly changed her mind when an explosion echoed through the night, and what in hell was *that*
about? She heard men screaming, more guns going off,
but so far—miracle of miracles—no slugs had struck the
car in which she sat.

That almost changed her mind, a small voice in her
head saying, *Stay here!*

"No way," she answered.

Had she already lost her mind? Garcelle decided she
would leave that worry for another time. Right now, the
one thing she was focused on was getting out of here alive.

She found the latch at last, yanked it, and threw her
weight backward against the door. It gave and nearly
spilled her to the pavement, as a dome light flared above
her, telling anyone nearby that she was on the move.

"Damn!"

She rolled out of the Mercury, landed on all fours, and
reached up to shut the door, hoping that Channer's men
were all too busy fighting for their lives to notice her.
Those men had come specifically to kill her, but there was
a chance her unknown rescuer would keep them busy long
enough for her to sneak away.

What did she owe a perfect stranger, after all?

Only her life.

That almost stopped her. Almost. But she told herself
she'd suffered through enough already, and she couldn't
help the stranger, being unarmed herself. Police were
bound to show up any minute, and the last thing Garcelle
needed was to wind up in a jail cell.

No. She was definitely running. It was every man—or *woman*—for themselves.

Garcelle began crawling toward the nearest cover, some tall trees, the nearest of them about fifty feet away. She could duck behind them, scramble to her feet and run, if no one cut her down before she reached them. A bullet struck the pavement near her left foot, stinging Garcelle's calf with asphalt shrapnel.

Move!

Throwing caution to the wind, she vaulted to her feet and ran as if her life depended on it—which, in fact, it might.

No warning shouts behind her. That was good, at least. If she could get a head start on whoever tried to follow her, maybe she could lose them in the dark. If not...well, it was better than remaining in the stranger's car, a stationary target.

Garcelle slammed into a solid body. She recoiled from the impact, lost her balance and fell back to the ground.

One of the Rasta goons stood over her, leering, his automatic weapon aimed at Garcelle's face.

"And where do you think you're goin'?"

FOUR MEN HAD MANAGED to escape the third car, all moving well enough despite the shot Bolan had fired to stop their progress. He didn't know if that meant he'd missed the driver, or if they'd begun with five men in the vehicle, but Bolan had no time to work out the specifics.

All four had to die.

They hadn't seen him yet, but they were moving in, holding a kind of skirmish line formation as they scuttled through the shadows, dodging lighted areas as best they could. It didn't help much, since he had them spotted from the start, but stopping them required a measure of finesse, to keep the fight from tipping into chaos.

Bolan took the point man first, a clean shot through the chest that sat him down and left him slumped there, his shoulder supported by a hedge he'd probably hoped would cover his advance.

The other three had seen their comrade drop, and while they couldn't tell precisely where the killing shot had come from, they immediately laid down fire to sweep the nearby shadows. Bolan was beyond their killing radius, so far, and seized the opportunity to drop a second gunman, double-tapping him from thirty yards to plant him facedown on the unforgiving pavement.

The remaining two were close to losing it. He saw it in their jerky movements. He heard it in the curses they were flinging at an unseen enemy and their random fire into the night. He stitched them with a short burst, half his Steyr's magazine exhausted now, and watched them fall together in a snarl of flaccid arms and legs.

That left the girl and who else, still alive on Bolan's killing field?

He went to find her, didn't have that far to look before he saw the posse gunman looming over her and grinning like he'd just unwrapped the greatest Christmas present ever.

The range—some forty yards—was nothing for his rifle or its telescopic sight. Backlit by floodlights from the parking lot, the posse thug was perfectly positioned for a clean shot through the head, chest, any part of him that Bolan chose. Playing it safe, he aimed for center mass and stroked the Steyr's trigger once, sending a 5.56 mm mangler downrange and closing the gap in less time than a heartbeat required.

The Rasta shooter toppled over backward, slowly, like a falling tree, and hit the pavement with a solid sound, skull thumping asphalt. Bolan scanned the killing ground for any further opposition, then moved to help the woman stand, gripping her arm.

"If this is where you want to stay," he said, "it's fine with me."

She seemed to think about it for a second, then shook her head. "No."

"Okay, then. We should get a move on."

He released her and walked back to the Mercury, the woman following a step or two behind. Still considering if she should bolt? He gave her all the room she needed, but she climbed into the shotgun seat beside him as he slid behind the steering wheel.

Bolan twisted the ignition key, gunning the Marauder's engine. "Guess I should introduce myself," he said. "Matt Cooper."

"I'm Garcelle. But you know that, of course."

"Do I?"

She blinked at that. "My father sent you…did he not?"

"Afraid I've never met the man," Bolan replied.

"I do not understand."

"I found you by coincidence," he said. "A lucky break."

"Unbelievable," she said. "I thought… So, you're a policeman?"

"Strike two."

"But, then…?"

Leaving the parking lot and rolling west, he said, "Start with your name."

"Garcelle. Garcelle Brouard."

And suddenly, it all made sense. "Which means your father would be—"

"Jean Brouard."

Top Haitian gangster in South Florida, perhaps in the United States. And yeah, it all made perfect sense now.

Bolan had come looking for a war, and he'd dropped into the middle of it, picking up a prize that might prove useful—or turn out to be a deadly albatross around his neck.

3

Richmond Heights, Kendall, Florida

The doctor wasn't licensed in America, although he'd had a thriving practice in Jamaica. He'd been arrested for trafficking in Class A drugs, served three years and was stripped of his professional credentials…before he was forgotten by the state. No one in Kingston missed him when he'd slipped away to Florida—at the suggestion of the Viper Posse—to help in situations such as this one.

"You will live," he told his patient. "I have stopped the bleeding and repaired the tissue damage. I am pleased to say the bullet missed your humerus and caused no damage to the shoulder socket."

Winston Channer, groggy from the pain and drugs he'd been given, answered, "Damn! It hurts like hell!"

"That's to be expected. These bullets tumble inside tissue, as you may know, and—"

"Stop the double-talk! What about my arm?"

The doctor frowned. "If you're careful with it, if you rest and follow my directions, you will probably regain full use of your arm."

"Probably? What do you mean, probably?"

"As I was trying to explain—"

"You damned quack! I'm going!"

He rose, fighting the sudden dizziness. Two of his soldiers came forward to support him as he rolled off the table and found his unsteady footing. Behind Channer, the doctor seemed about to panic. "You must rest!" he warned. "Your blood loss—"

"You'll lose blood, if you don't shut your mouth!"

The doctor backed away, nodding in resignation.

"Gimme a phone!" he ordered no one in particular. Both of his men extended cell phones, and he took one, opened it, began to dial.

"Who ya callin, Boss?" one dared to ask.

"Gordon. We shoulda heard from him by now."

The call went straight to voice mail, ramping Channer's fury up another notch. "Damn! Where is he?"

"He hasn't called, Boss," one of Channer's soldiers said.

"I know that! I woulda talked to him if he'd called."

He was about to close the phone and hand it back when it surprised him with a chirping tone. Channer almost dropped it, let another ring pass while considering if he should give the cell back to its owner, then decided he would answer it himself.

"What?"

On the other end, a voice he recognized asked, "Germaine? Where's the boss?"

"You're talkin' to him. Did you find 'em?"

Hesitation on the line, before the caller answered, "They're dead, Boss."

"What? Who's dead?"

"Those boys, all of them."

"*What?*" Channer repeated, feeling foolish. "That can't be right."

"It's true. I seen 'em myself, and Babylon's all over there."

"Damn it! Did they kill the white man?"

"Didn't see him, Boss."

"What about the woman?"

"She's not here."

Snarling an incoherent curse, Channer switched off the cell and tossed it from him. Someone caught it, tucked it in a pocket and was wise enough to ask no questions.

"All our brothers are dead," he told them. His wounded arm throbbed—the local anesthetic wearing off—which only worsened Channer's mood. "How could one man do all that?"

When no one answered, Channer decided on his own. "He couldn't do it! It's impossible."

"He must've had help," one of his soldiers offered.

"This shit isn't finished," Channer said. "I'm gonna find this bastard and he's gonna say who sent him."

"And the woman?" asked his other bodyguard.

"She's run home to her papa," Channer replied. "Where else?"

"Good thinkin', Boss."

"I'm gonna hear this white man screaming out his lungs. He'll beg to die before I'm done."

One of the soldiers cleared his throat and asked, "You gonna tell the Don, Boss?"

Damn! Channer had almost let that aspect of the problem slip his fevered mind. His master would be waiting for a call in Kingston, and he couldn't stall much longer.

"Of course," he replied. "I'll call him soon as I find the scrambler phone."

"I've got it," said the soldier to his left, reaching inside his jacket.

Channer could have slapped him, but he took the phone instead and switched on its scrambler, waiting for the green light to stop flashing and burn steadily. When it was ready, he speed-dialed the only number in its memory.

Nearly six hundred miles away, a grim voice answered on the second ring. "What's happening?"

"I'm sorry, Boss," he said. "I've got bad news."

Briar Bay Park, Kendall, Florida

BOLAN HAD PARKED his Mercury and sat there in the dark with Garcelle Brouard. She had declined medical treatment and agreed to speak with him before he dropped her off, her final destination still unspecified.

"So, Channer picked you up to strike a blow against your father," Bolan said.

Garcelle nodded. "I'm not sure if he expected to collect a ransom or dispose of me. Either way, he misjudged my father."

"Your father wouldn't miss you? Wouldn't pay to get you back?"

"I cannot say how he might feel if I was dead," Garcelle replied. "I like to think he'd mourn, of course, but that may be wishful thinking. As for paying ransom? Never. It would set a precedent that he could not abide."

Clearly, she was an educated woman, not the standard mobster's daughter raised on perks and privilege.

He changed tacks. "Are you sure about the hospital?"

"I'm fine," she said, raising a hand to lightly touch her swollen lower lip. "You came—how do they say it—in the nick of time?"

"That's how they say it. Were they grilling you about your father's business?"

"Trying to, but there was nothing I could tell them. From the time I was born, I've been excluded from that side of Papa's life. It was important to him, I believe, to have a semblance of a normal family. As if that's even possible."

He heard a note of bitterness in Garcelle's voice and followed up on it. "I guess it isn't easy on your mother, either."

"I suppose it wasn't, but she died when I was four years old. Was murdered, I should say. A business rival of my father's set a bomb, and… It was difficult for me to understand, at first. I missed her, as you may imagine. Papa never remarried, although whether out of loyalty to Mama's memory or to avoid another incident, I couldn't say. There were tutors, and a governess."

"We've all lost people," Bolan said, remembering his parents and his younger sister, lives cut short by the Mafia intrigue that launched his never ending war.

"That's true, of course. The past five years, I've been away at school in Paris. Papa thought I would be safe there." With the bare trace of a wicked smile, she added, "If he only knew."

"And now, you're back."

"Six weeks ago. It took that long for Channer's men to find me, I suppose."

"Where will you go now?" Bolan asked.

"Back to Papa, first, to put his mind at ease. From there, I would imagine he'll send me off again. As long as it's not Haiti, I'm content."

"Not homesick, then?"

"You've been to Haiti?"

"On occasion."

"Then you know the answer to your question. While my family has never suffered poverty, at least within my lifetime, Haiti is a pit of misery and crime. That must sound quite ironic, eh?"

"Well… Men like your father haven't exactly helped make things better."

"Of course. And, as you can see, I've taken full advantage of his filthy money."

"It's a choice," Bolan acknowledged. "You're well educated. You could make your own way in the world."

"Blood tells, as the saying goes. Also a song, I believe."

Bolan wasn't a preacher. He dropped it. "So, where should I take you?"

"I have a friend in Coral Gables, if it's not too far out of your way."

He estimated twenty minutes on South Dixie Highway, give or take.

"Sounds good," Bolan replied, and fired up the Marauder's mill.

Windward Road, Kingston, Jamaica

JEROME QUARRIE HAD NEVER learned to take bad news in stride. He'd been trying, lately, to control his temper. It was sheer folly, in the midst of war, to kill his men each time they disappointed him.

The way things had been going lately, he'd have no soldiers left.

And so he listened, teeth clenched, to the story of pathetic failure Winston Channer told him. Nineteen soldiers dead, seven at Kingston House, and twelve lost in pursuit of the mysterious white man who staged the raid. It was a grave loss, nearly ten percent of Quarrie's whole Miami garrison, but what infuriated him the most was losing the woman.

His hostage.

Channer had stopped talking. Quarrie took a deep breath, tried counting to ten as he'd been advised, but only got to five.

"All those brothers dead, but you're still livin'."

"I nearly lost my arm."

"I find out this is your fault," Quarrie said, "you're gonna lose your head."

"Boss, I didn't—"

"Shut up!" Quarrie said. "Find the woman and the man who snatched her from you. Kill the two of them and bring me proof. You can't do that, I'll do the job myself, and then kill you. Understand?"

"All right, Boss." Relief was audible in Channer's voice. "It's all good. I miss, I'm dead."

"Remember that," Quarrie replied, and cut the link.

He reached for some rum and ganja, for the maximum effect. One scorched his throat, the other seeped into his lungs and made his troubles seem, if not remote, at least a little more removed from his immediate concern. He had already given orders to be left alone, unless the house burst into flames, and even then he knew his men would hesitate to clamor for attention.

"I'm gonna drink your blood," he muttered to the unknown enemy, the man who'd appeared from nowhere, slaughtering his men and foiling Quarrie's scheme. "Don't think I'll forget. I won't stop until I pay you back for this."

Until the job was done.

Coral Gables, Florida

GARCELLE BROUARD HAD no friends in Coral Gables, but she did have an apartment on Granada Boulevard. The man who called himself Matt Cooper dropped her off, wished her well and drove away in his Mercury Marauder with its motor rumbling.

The doorman greeted her with all the courtesy her high-priced rent deserved, and he solemnly assured Garcelle that no one had come asking for her in her absence. Neither had there been reports of any lowlife gangster types lurking around the neighborhood. The very notion seemed outrageous and amusing, given the development's security precautions and its good relationship with the police.

Despite that reassurance, Garcelle exercised her usual degree of caution as she rode the elevator to her floor, one level underneath the penthouse occupied by the star of a TV show set in Miami. She checked the tiny scrap of paper that she wedged between the door and jamb each time she left, unnoticeable until it had been dislodged, and then impossible to put back in the same place once the door was opened. Only Garcelle knew the combination to the door's keypad. In the rare event of an emergency, firefighters would be forced to use an axe or pry bar to get in.

She let herself inside, then instantly secured the two dead bolts before she searched the flat, armed with a pistol she kept in the kitchen. There was another wedged between the cushions of her sofa, and a third in Garcelle's nightstand. One of many things she'd learned from Papa: always be prepared.

It was embarrassing that she'd been taken by surprise, out on the street, but she was home now, relatively safe—a concept more or less devoid of meaning in the present circumstance—and it was time to let her father know that she'd escaped. As to how much she'd tell him, Garcelle knew the answer.

Everything.

She'd lost her cell phone to the Viper Posse, but it didn't matter. Garcelle grabbed the cordless from the kitchen, took it with her as she roamed through the apartment, checking every room and closet, stopping down to peer beneath the bed. When she was satisfied at last, she sat down on the bed, two guns beside her now, and dialed her father's number. Abner Biassou took the call, her father's second in command.

"Hello."

"Abner, I need to speak with Papa."

"Miss, are you—"

"I'm fine. Just put him on."

Another moment passed before her father's voice came on the line.

"I'm sorry, my dear, but I cannot—"

"Negotiate with kidnappers?" She laughed at him. "Of course not, Father."

"But—"

"That's why I had no choice but to escape."

"You're free? Where are you? How did you—"

"Not now," she interrupted. "This line's not secure."

"Of course. But I must still know where you are, to send protection."

"I'm at home and safe for now. But if you'd care to send a car…"

"I'll send a caravan," her father said. "A convoy."

"Nothing quite so obvious."

"Two cars, then. I insist."

"That should be more than adequate."

"You constantly surprise me, child."

"There are more surprises waiting, when I see you."

"Oh?"

"Indeed."

"Good news, or bad?" he asked.

"I'm not sure yet."

"I am intrigued."

"You must be patient for a little longer."

"Lock your doors, and—"

"I know what I'm doing. Goodbye, Father."

She cut the link, cradled the cordless phone and spent the next ten minutes packing what she needed for a stay away from home. Cosmetics were not a priority, but she packed clothes, two extra pairs of shoes and every document she could think of: her driver's license, passport, birth certificate professionally altered to present her as a native-born American, and so on.

Garcelle packed her three pistols, as well. There was no point in leaving them behind for an intruder to discover. Two of the guns were Glock 19 Compacts, both perfectly reliable and efficient, but her favorite was the Heckler

& Koch P2000 SK, a sub-compact model that weighed only twenty-four ounces while packing ten hollow-point rounds. Garcelle was proficient with all three weapons, but she'd never shot a man.

Since her experience with Channer's thugs, she hoped—not for the first time—that she might be favored with the chance to find out what it felt like.

All in due time, she decided, and was ready when the buzzer rang from downstairs, the doorman announcing that her escorts had arrived. She took her rolling bag, two guns inside it and the P2000 SK in her purse, and left her comfortable flat, perhaps for good. If she did not return, so be it. Finding new accommodations would not be a problem.

She was more concerned about survival at the moment.

And revenge.

FROM CORAL GABLES, Bolan traveled north to Miami Shores, a stretch of waterfront abutting Biscayne Bay. Here, the Viper Posse made their presence felt by dealing drugs while skirmishing with the gangs that had preceded them, as well as latecomers who'd claimed a slice of turf after the fact.

His target was another posse hangout, this one called Armagideon, a Rasta variation on the final clash of good and evil from the Book of Revelation.

Bolan parked a block down range, on Northeast 96th Street. He locked up the Marauder and took the Steyr AUG and pistols with him as he walked down to the club, scanning the street along his way for any lookouts. He saw none and wondered if word of his first clash with Channer's minions hadn't reached the village yet, or if the soldiers here had chosen to ignore it.

Either way, they were about to get a wake-up call.

As he approached the club, Bolan heard its roof-mounted air conditioner kick into life, its droning loud enough to cover him as he tried the front door's knob. It turned and Bolan slipped inside, his silenced rifle up and ready to meet any challenge from within, but no one stopped him as he cleared a smallish entryway and moved along a short hall, toward the sound of reggae music. He had nearly reached a curtain made of colored beads when the expected outer guard appeared, clutching a sandwich in his right hand, a beer bottle in his left.

The shock of being confronted by a man with a gun immobilized his adversary for a crucial second. Bolan took advantage of it, squeezing off a single shot that drilled the hungry man's chest and punched him backward through the rattling curtain, toward the strains of island rhythm. Bolan followed, arriving just as the dead man's companions registered his body flopping on the floor.

Four of them leaped up from a card table where they'd been playing poker; two more bolted from a bar on Bolan's right, reaching for weapons hidden underneath their baggy tie-dyed shirts. A seventh posse member was behind the bar, cracking a beer, but he dropped it when he noticed the intruder and his automatic rifle.

Time does not slow down in combat. Quite the opposite, in fact. When the smoke clears, survivors may have only fragmentary memories of what they did, or who they killed, in order to survive. Bolan, thanks to his long experience, saw everything that happened with a perfect clarity, but had no images of slow-mo tumbling corpses, bottles shattering artistically behind the bar, or any other tricks well-known from Hollywood.

It was an ugly business, killing, and he did it very well.

He had the Steyr set for 3-round bursts and made them count, beginning with the guy behind the bar, who had more cover and was reaching for a weapon. That target fell, surrounded by a drifting mist of blood, as Bolan turned to work the room, tracking from left to right and nailing others as they came. When he finished, there were nine rounds left in his translucent magazine, and pools of blood were spreading on the vinyl-covered floor, merging to form a single crimson lake. Of seven adversaries, only one had fired a shot, and that was wasted on the ceiling.

When no one else appeared, Bolan took the time to move behind the bar and smash a number of the rum and whiskey bottles shelved there. Then he ignited their dribbling contents to produce a wall of hungry, hissing flame. He saw no sprinkler system—tag them with a violation of the building safety code—which would allow the fire to spread, and maybe find its way upstairs before some passerby raised an alarm.

You wanted Armagideon, he thought. So, here it is.

4

Liberty City, Miami

Winston Channer had gone to ground in Miami's ghetto, surrounded by guards in a small house two blocks from Sherdavia Jenkins Peace Park. He had no idea who Sherdavia was, didn't know his or her story, and did not care to hear it. Another victim of the race war, he assumed, whose pain could not compare with the throbbing ache in his arm and shoulder.

Or the aching in his head, after he took the second bad-news call that night.

A fire at Armagideon, with eight more soldiers dead, apparently cut down before they could defend themselves. He cursed the men who'd let him down, together with the man or men who'd killed them, wishing they all stood before him now, and he could be the one who slaughtered them. A cane knife would be good for that. Perhaps a chain saw.

Channer had been on the verge of calling Quarrie back, then stopped himself. His master clearly did not wish to hear from him until he'd atoned for his failures by killing or capturing Garcelle Brouard and the white man who'd rescued her—whoever he might be. Channer still had no clue on that score, nor the first idea of where he should begin his search.

The pain meds helped, but Channer had begun to think they might dull his senses. Unfortunately, the drugs couldn't erase his present worries—or the threat of agonizing death, if Quarrie thought Channer had failed him. He was trapped, it seemed, between one madman and another, with his only way to safety being *through* one or the other. And if Channer had to choose, he'd pick the white man as his adversary every time.

So far, he'd imagined three distinct angles of attack. The first, hunting Garcelle Brouard, began with checking every place she was known to frequent. A team of soldiers was on the way to raid her flat, and if they didn't find her there, they had a short list of alternatives to check. His men had been cautioned to leave no witnesses who could identify them to police.

The second avenue was using Channer's contacts in local law enforcement, officers who valued cash over their oath of office. That only helped him if the cops captured the white man he was searching for. It was always possible—though, frankly, he considered it unlikely.

Finally, he could go after Jean Brouard directly, in a bid to prove himself once and for all. The hostage ploy had failed, but he might be able to eliminate Brouard before the Haitian mobster launched a full-scale retaliation toward the Viper Posse. That would be a victory Quarrie could not ignore. Channer would be in line for a promotion, maybe elevation to a high rank in the posse, back in Kingston.

Not that he was anxious to depart from Florida, or the United States in general.

Channer had been born and raised on a small island, in the depths of poverty, and he relished every moment he spent in plush American society. Even the country's ghettos were a great improvement on the slums of Kingston, where he'd once roamed the streets like a wild animal, committing petty thefts to feed himself. Today, at home, he would be envied by the yardie boys still fighting to establish reputations.

But he was not satisfied.

Channer craved wealth beyond his wildest dreams— and, he admitted to himself, his dreams were truly wild. He'd watched *Scarface* twenty-seven times, so far, and memorized the layout of Tony Montana's vast mansion, his fleet of sleek cars, not to mention the arsenal stashed in his closet.

If he could kill Jean Brouard, crush his clique in Miami and capture his turf, Channer would have no further use for Quarrie, sitting back at home in Kingston. He could call the shots, become a legend in his own young lifetime. All he had to do was strike without remorse, eradicate his enemies and claim the city as his own.

GARCELLE BROUARD HAD left Haiti hoping she'd never be reminded of it again, but here she was in Little Haiti, a hostage of her father's stubborn refusal to leave the old ways behind. He could easily afford a mansion—even two or three—in South Beach, on Fisher Island or nearby Star Island, but he remained in the old neighborhood, albeit living in a degree of luxury unknown to most of Little Haiti's inhabitants, insisting that proximity kept him in touch with the things that mattered.

Now, after hours in captivity, Garcelle was coming "home" to a place she despised.

Armed guards were waiting when she stepped out of the black Lincoln Navigator. One took her bag and the others surrounded her, escorting her into the house while neighbors peered from their windows. She couldn't stop them gawking at her, or prevent them from phoning Winston Channer to report her whereabouts, but she believed her father's reputation would make the greediest among them hesitate before betraying him.

They knew the grim price of disloyalty.

Inside the house, thank heavens, it smelled nothing like the streets. Her father was particular about the air-conditioning, to keep away the damp, mold and pervasive odors of the neighborhood. It couldn't always scrub the air completely clean, but on this night, after her near miss with the Viper Posse, Garcelle found the atmosphere relaxing and invigorating, all at once.

"My beautiful daughter," her father said. The bodyguards stood back, their eyes averted, as his arms enfolded her. "I was afraid I might never see you in this world again, or else, that we would have our last reunion at the morgue."

"Worried for nothing, Papa. Here I am."

"But not without some help, I understand."

Garcelle surveyed the men surrounding them and said, "We should discuss that privately."

"Of course." Her father gestured to the guards and told them, "Leave us." They left immediately, without speaking.

When the door had closed behind them, Garcelle said, "It was a white man. Have you heard?"

Her father frowned. "Who was he?"

Garcelle shrugged. "He calls himself Matt Cooper. I assume it's short for Matthew, but…"

"You don't believe him."

"Why should I? By my count, he killed more than a dozen men tonight, with no attempt at first arresting them."

"It's double that or more, by now," her father said. "Your white man, or another, has been busy since he left you."

"All against the Viper Posse?"

"So far."

"Then he's doing our work for us," she replied.

Her father shrugged. "Perhaps. I would feel better if he left us, all the same."

"Perhaps I can arrange that."

"Oh?"

"He has invited me to call him, if I need his help."

"And do you? Need him?"

Garcelle smiled. "I might."

Country Walk, Dade County, Florida

THE VIPER POSSE HAD set up shop on Southwest 141st Street. They didn't have an office per se, just a house where they stashed guns and crack cocaine, bedrooms converted to a barracks for the soldiers left to guard the merchandise. Neighbors were wise enough to keep their mouths shut, for the most part, after one suspicious fire claimed a family of four. That case was still unsolved, but Bolan didn't do investigations of the legal kind.

He got the facts then acted on them, cutting out a slew of useless middlemen.

As he was acting now.

GPS led Bolan to the neighborhood he wanted, and he saw no suspicious lurkers at the target address on his drive-by.

Wishful thinking on the posse's part? Or had they bailed out on receiving news of Bolan's other recent raids?

There was only one way to find out.

Light rain was falling as he parked the Mercury Marauder and went EVA, the Steyr riding easy on a shoulder sling beneath his thin raincoat. A Tilley hat in olive drab kept the drizzle out of his eyes and shadowed his face as he passed beneath streetlights, walking a long block to his target.

Still no guards outside, but music was coming from the house, and the windows at the back were lit. Bolan couldn't tell if they were partying inside, or mourning for their lately fallen comrades. Either way, they were distracted, which made his job easier.

He stopped and whistled softly at a backyard gate, waiting to see if any dogs appeared, and entered when they didn't. The Bermuda grass back there was ankle high, in need of mowing, but it clearly wasn't a priority. It wet his shoes and trouser cuffs as Bolan walked around behind the house, to reach a screened-in porch where light and tunes were spilling from an open back door.

Three posse goons were lounging on the porch, passing a joint around, before he stepped out of the night to startle them. One of them cried out and bolted to his feet, so high on ganja that he stumbled as he turned and tried to reach an automatic rifle propped against the wall, behind his wicker chair. The other two were slower on the uptake, rising from their seats with awkward, lurching moves as Bolan brought them under fire.

The Steyr spat its nearly silent 3-round bursts, catching the first man up below his shoulder blade, mangling his lung and heart before he did a solid face plant on the porch's decking. Bolan swung around to catch the others drawing handguns, sent one's Rasta cap flying with half of his skull still inside it, and pulverized the other's sternum, dropping him onto a small glass-topped table that shattered beneath him.

A heartbeat later, he was through the flapping screen door and inside the house, catching another groggy member of the posse blinking at him from a ratty sofa. Bolan killed him where he sat and moved on, past the thumping stereo, in search of other prey. He found none but did turn up a suitcase filled with little bags of rock in one of the four bedrooms. Bolan took it to the kitchen, emptied it onto the burners of a Frigidaire gas range and turned the burners on. He cleared the room before the plastic melted and the crack began to sizzle, breaking down.

The last he'd heard, crack sold on the streets for around forty dollars per quarter-gram—call it one hundred sixty thousand dollars per kilogram to the junkies who smoked it. The suitcase had weighed thirteen kilograms, minimum, so that was better than two million dollars sizzling on the stovetop behind him, filling the kitchen with poisonous fumes. Not a fortune, to dealers, but something.

On his way out, Bolan stopped and set fire to the living room curtains, waiting till they caught and sent flames leaping toward the ceiling. Finished, he retreated the way he'd come, through the gate and along the street, back to his car.

Already thinking of the next stop on his blitzkrieg trail and wondering, in one small corner of his mind, about Garcelle Brouard.

Southwest 117th Avenue, Northbound

BOLAN WAS ON HIS WAY to hit a Tamiami whorehouse when his cell phone vibrated. Checking his rearview mirror for patrol cars, he retrieved it from a pocket and took the call.

"Hello?"

"Is that you, Mr. Cooper? Matt?"

He was surprised to hear from her, much less so soon after he'd dropped her in Coral Gables. "Any trouble?" he inquired, not using names.

"There might be." Garcelle sounded anxious. Not unexpected, after her recent experience, but was there something more to it?

"What's the problem?" he inquired.

"I tried to reach my father, but I can't get hold of him."

"Is that unusual?"

"Very. There's always someone with a number or an address."

"It's been hectic," he reminded her. "Maybe he's lying low."

"He does not hide from me."

"I've got my hands full," Bolan said. "There's not much I can do for you right now."

"Not much? Or nothing?"

He thought about it for a second and said, "There might be someplace I could take you, but I'd have to make some calls."

"I *knew* you wouldn't let me down."

"Don't count on anything," he cautioned her. "It could go either way."

"Of course."

"And if you're taken in, there may be questions."

"About Channer?"

"And your father."

"Ah. Well, that's all right. I never wanted any part of that life."

"Are you sure?"

"You don't know how often I've tried to break away from him."

"That means a change in everything you know and take for granted," Bolan said.

"A change is what I need," Garcelle replied.

"Okay. Give me your number there. I'll call you back."

She rattled off nine digits. He repeated them, committing them to memory. "Stay there," he said, at last. "I don't know how long this will take."

"Please hurry," Garcelle urged, and cut the link.

Stowing his cell, he wondered what was going on in Garcelle's mind. Her father dropping out of touch might rattle her, but would it turn her into an informant, just like that? Was this the break she'd been waiting for? Or was something else at work, behind the scenes?

It might, he realized, turn out to be a trap. He didn't know the lady well enough to judge her heart or mind, could only say for sure that she'd been raised in luxury, on blood money, for twenty-something years. Had she attempted to escape the family before? Was she sincere now, or was it a sham?

He'd make the necessary calls, get back to her as soon as possible, but Bolan wasn't sending anybody else to make the pickup when the time came. If a trap was waiting for him, he alone would step into it and respond accordingly. A two-front war was fine with Bolan. Truth be told, he preferred it.

He'd start with Hal, explain the situation and his doubts and ask for a referral to the FBI or United States Marshals Service in Miami, someone Hal knew well enough to trust. His second call would wake whoever Hal had recommended, and he'd tell the story once again, redacted to include only the bare essentials. If the case agent agreed—and it was possible that he or she would not—Bolan would call Garcelle back to arrange a pickup.

And if something led Hal's contact to refuse? What, then?

Bolan would think of something, do whatever he could manage for Garcelle, without putting his mission on the line. He had a job to do, and it took precedence over the rescue of a mobster's daughter. Her father was a target, though a secondary one, and there was still a chance he'd have to orphan her before he wrapped Miami and moved on.

But he would try to get her out alive, if she'd let him.

And if it turned out he couldn't trust her...well, the lady would be on her own.

Little Haiti, Miami

THE CALLBACK CAME within twenty-five minutes. Garcelle picked up on the first ring, her stomach aflutter, which pleased her unexpectedly. Emotion, though it could be detrimental if allowed to run unchecked, was sometimes a sweet fringe benefit of doing business.

"Matthew?" Just the right tone of anxiety, she thought, a little breathless.

"We have contact," Bolan said. "I need a time and place for pickup."

"Who will I be meeting?"

"Me. The handoff follows afterward."

"It sounds very…impersonal." Too coy? She was afraid she might have overplayed her hand.

Cooper sidestepped it, telling her, "You'll be secure. I don't have any other details for you."

Putting on a pouty face, although he could not see it through the telephone, she said, "As long as you'll be meeting me."

"That's what I said."

Was there an edge to Cooper's voice? Did he suspect something? No matter. She'd planned the rest of it and had a script to follow.

"I was thinking you could pick me up at Williams Park," she said. "Do you know where that is?"

"Northwest 17th Street," he replied, surprising her. "Near Overtown."

"Exactly. There's a bus stop by the baseball field, the southeast corner of the park where 17th Street intersects Northwest 4th Avenue."

"I'll be there," Bolan said. "How long?"

"I'll need the best part of an hour," Garcelle told him.

"See you then." And he was gone.

"A man of few words," her father observed. He was

seated on the far end of the sofa. He'd been silent as she spoke to Cooper and was frowning now. "Do you think he suspects anything?"

"Why would he?"

A casual shrug. "Men like this, the survivors, take nothing for granted, Garcelle."

"Was I not convincing?"

"Personally, I would say your performance was above reproach. You must be careful, nonetheless."

"I always am."

"I wish that were the case," he said. "But you were captured by our enemies, if you recall."

"I'm not likely to forget it."

"Which created the present situation," he went on, as if she hadn't spoken. "Now, I ask if you are ready to proceed, or if I should arrange a substitute for your protection."

"Substitute?"

"We need a woman at the meeting who resembles you on casual inspection. If I sent Monique—"

"Monique does not resemble me!"

"She's close enough to serve as bait. She also has experience in matters of this kind."

"You don't think I can do the job, Father?"

He answered with a question of his own. "Am I correct in thinking that you have not killed a man before?"

"Not yet."

"To start with someone so experienced, who also saved your life, might be considered…problematic."

"It's no problem for me."

"You're sure of that? Quite certain?"

"Absolutely. Let me prove myself to you."

"No proof of this sort is required. I give you everything you need."

That line again. "I want to *earn* my way," she told him, feeling anger warm her cheeks.

"This man might kill you. Then what shall I do, without an heir?"

"As I've suspected all along, Father. You'll simply live forever."

"Ah. If only that were possible."

"Let me do this. I promise not to disappoint you."

He was slowly yielding. "Very well," he said. "But under Abner's supervision."

"I don't need—"

"It's settled. My terms, or I send Monique."

"An offer I cannot refuse?"

"The only kind worth making."

Garcelle forced a smile. "In that case, I agree. And I must hurry, or I'll miss him."

"That *would* be a disappointment. Watch your back, daughter."

"I always do," she said, and left him sitting by himself.

It rankled that her father didn't trust her fully with a simple task, but she supposed his doubt was unavoidable. He was a chauvinist, of course, unlikely to outgrow it at his age. He knew women were capable of killing—take that bitch Monique, for instance—but he didn't wish to think the stains on his hands were inherited.

Too bad. For once, she was about to teach her father something.

And he would ignore the lesson at his peril.

5

Williams Park, Miami

Bolan rolled past St. Peter's Antiochian Orthodox Church, southbound on Northwest 4th Court, toward the park. He was early but didn't have time for the thorough recon he would have preferred. Ahead of him, the park was cloaked in darkness, none of its floodlights blazing over the baseball field.

At this hour, the park was deserted—or so it would seem. He followed the road he was on through a curve to the west, driving past the basketball courts and a small parking lot to catch Northwest 5th Avenue southbound. He was supposed to meet Garcelle Brouard at a bus stop, but the whole block was lined with trees that could shelter snipers—if the meeting was a trap.

Why would she play it that way?

Bolan didn't know, but he'd learned you can't truly understand another person's mind or heart on short acquaintance. Allies had betrayed him in the past, with terrible results. Why should he trust a total stranger, just because he'd stumbled across her in a vulnerable moment and had saved her life?

Instead of driving past the bus stop, Bolan parked in the deserted lot of Town Park, opposite the scheduled rendezvous location. The smaller park was even darker than its neighbor, an invitation to nefarious deeds, but he had the lot to himself as he switched off the Marauder's engine and prepared to go from there on foot.

She wouldn't be expecting that. Neither would anyone she might have brought along.

It didn't bother Bolan that Garcelle might try to have him killed or captured. He was well-informed about her family, its violent roots in Haiti.

Bolan was dressed for battle, wearing black from head to toe. Both sidearms were snugged in quick-draw holsters, with his Steyr AUG ready to rock and roll. He hoped the precaution was unnecessary, but experience had taught him that a soldier usually died because of something he'd failed to do, an underestimation of his enemies.

And Jean Brouard *was* Bolan's enemy. He'd planned on shaking up the Haitian mob while he was in Miami, maybe using them against the Viper Posse if the opportunity arose. Now, thanks to a coincidence, he had to treat the outfit as a clear and present threat.

Or, on the other hand, perhaps Garcelle would play it straight.

The odds? Bolan could not have said.

And if the lady had betrayed him? What, then?

Bolan was practical. He didn't draw a line at killing women, if they posed a mortal threat to him or others. Enemies were enemies, regardless of their gender, race, or creed.

He hoped Garcelle would not be one of those, but if she'd laid a snare for him, she'd have to take her chances with the Executioner.

ABNER BIASSOU HATED WAITING. He'd always been an action-oriented guy. He took what he wanted when he wanted it and messed up anyone who tried to stop him. Now, of course, he was a captain with responsibility. Which made it all the more irksome to be staked out in darkness, lying on his belly with a rifle at his side, watching the boss's daughter sitting at a bus stop in the middle of the night.

For what?

As Abner understood it, some white man had saved Garcelle from almost certain death—torture at least, since the Viper Posse was renowned for it—and had annihilated twenty-odd of Winston Channer's men. He thought they should be cheering the anonymous commando, standing back to let him wipe out Channer and the other Kingston sons of whores rather than assassinating him.

Why help the enemy by taking out a man hell-bent on killing them? It made no sense.

But Papa Jean had not consulted him. It was his way to issue orders, and subordinates who failed to execute them properly would feel his wrath. Biassou had received instructions to eliminate the white man, and his sole response had been *Yes, sir.*

He hadn't come alone, of course. Considering the stranger's prowess, Abner had handpicked seven men to join him on the stakeout, each a proven killer who'd served with Haiti's army or its national police. Not simpleminded grunts, but men who'd seen it all, from grilling prisoners to riot duty and eliminating opposition at election time.

The members of his team were similarly armed, each with an automatic weapon and at least one pistol, all connected to Biassou by their wireless headsets, ready to receive his orders when the time was right.

Assuming the white man even showed.

Garcelle appeared to think she had the stranger at her beck and call, although she'd only met him briefly and couldn't really claim to know the man at all. He had agreed to meet her, some scheme about protective custody, but Abner thought it was a fifty-fifty shot that he would change his mind, decide she wasn't worth the trouble.

After all, he *did* have other things to do.

The Viper Posse had been wounded, but it still survived. Garcelle was a distraction. Would a true professional allow himself to be diverted from a mission by a stranger's plea for help?

Biassou checked his Rolex watch. Garcelle's savior had five minutes left before they had to mark him down as tardy.

Abner had inquired how long they ought to linger in the park, if he was late. He'd asked the boss, refusing to accept Garcelle as his commander, even though he treated her with all due honor. Papa Jean had ordered that they wait for half an hour, making an allowance for the white man getting lost or stuck in traffic. They could pull out then, if he hadn't arrived, and take Garcelle back home.

Biassou hoped the night might end that way. He didn't like to see a woman rising to direct the family, no matter if she was intelligent and coldhearted. Crime was a man's world, and he wanted it to stay that way.

How else could Abner hope to claim his due as leader of the syndicate, when Death eventually called on Papa Jean?

A movement on the far side of the street alerted him. Was that a figure in the shadows, peering at Garcelle?

"Wake up," he whispered to his men. "We may have something here."

GARCELLE BROUARD WAS NERVOUS. This waiting on the street had started to unnerve her—which, in turn, had made her irritable, angry at herself. She hated those feelings, but found that tonight, she couldn't control them.

Waiting sucked.

Garcelle was starting to second-guess herself, and that was not a quality of leadership. She listened for Biassou's warning, wondered whether he would spot Cooper before she did—or if the man would even show at all.

He'll be here, she decided. Garcelle trusted him to that extent, and wondered if his trust in her was strong enough to lead him to his death.

What others would have seen as treachery, Garcelle viewed as a test of character. Her father was observing her, considering her argument that leadership of their criminal family should not be dependent on whether or not the leader possessed testicles. She had cajoled, debated, argued with her father for five years, at least, trying to make him see the light. Over the past twelve months, she'd noted cracks in his traditionalist facade, small signs of progress for her side. Tonight would show him she possessed the final quality required to help him lead.

"Making her bones," Italian mobsters called it, or were rumored to. Killing a man of Matthew Cooper's prowess, never mind his real name, would be vastly more impressive than eliminating some street thug who'd trespassed against the family. And killing him after he'd saved her life? That was the icing on the cake.

She listened for Biassou's warning, slipped a hand into the pocket of her raincoat, where the Heckler & Koch P2000 SK nestled snugly, a round in its chamber, ten in the clip. She carried two spare magazines, as well, but knew that if she needed them, she'd probably be dead before she could reload.

Cooper appeared to be a gentleman, for all his taciturnity, but Garcelle thought he wouldn't hesitate to kill her if she missed her own first shot. He might be soft where women were concerned, but he was not a fool.

Biassou's voice rasped in her ear. "Wake up. We may have something here."

No cars were coming. She looked across the street, toward Town Park. There, immersed in shadows cast by trees, she saw a human figure. Watching her? And if so, was it Cooper?

Criminals were known to haunt Miami's parks, like those of every other city. This could be a mugger, and she nearly smiled, thinking about the rude surprise he'd get if he attacked her at the bus stop. It would spoil the trap she'd laid for Cooper, sadly, but it might be fun.

The figure on the far side of the street was moving now, emerging from the shadows, stepping toward the curb. Cooper. Of course, it was. She saw him stop and look both ways, the way children were taught to do with traffic, but she knew his eyes were scanning Williams Park, looking for evidence that she'd betrayed him.

Then he began to cross the street.

BOLAN WAS HALFWAY across Northwest 17th Street when Garcelle rose from the bus stop bench and came to meet him on the sidewalk. She was smiling, seemed to have no luggage other than a purse over her shoulder, hands inside the pockets of a lightweight coat that stopped just above her knees.

"I was afraid you'd change your mind," she said.

Bolan kept looking past her, sharp eyes probing shadows. Nodding toward her shoulder bag, he asked, "That's all you're bringing?"

"It's enough," she said, losing the smile as she began to draw a pistol from her right-hand pocket.

Bolan had a fraction of a second to decide. He chose to let her live, butt-stroked her gun hand with the Steyr's polymer stock, using force enough to crack her wrist and send the weapon clattering across concrete. He lunged to grab her hair, wedged the rifle's silencer beneath her jaw and was just about to ask for an explanation when a shout went up from somewhere deeper in the park, behind the nearby screen of trees.

Men running, moving shadows in the deeper darkness. Bolan shoved Garcelle away from him. She stumbled, went down on her backside as he crouched and brought the auto rifle to his shoulder.

Muzzle-flashes made it easier for him to spot his enemies. The nearest of the gang was twenty yards away and closing, firing on the run, which spoiled his aim. Bolan triggered a 3-round burst that caught the shooter in midstride and knocked him backward, finger still clamped on his weapon's trigger, wasting bullets on the velvet sky and stars above.

One down, but now the others had begun to find their range. A streetlight halfway down the block worked against Bolan, and the open sidewalk offered him no cover. If he ran now, back across the empty two-lane road, he likely wouldn't make it to the smaller park, much less his waiting car.

So, stand and fight.

He counted seven shooters still in action, figured that was all of them. No one who wanted to impress the boss would hang back on the sidelines. Garcelle was crawling toward her pistol, ducking underneath the friendly fire. Bolan suppressed an urge to pick her off and focused on the soldiers who were closing in on him.

No time to wonder why she had betrayed him. Maybe it was simply in her blood. He made a mental note to call on Garcelle's daddy, if he lived that long, then got down to the brutal business of survival.

Soldier two had nearly reached the sidewalk when a second 3-round burst from Bolan's AUG stitched him above the belt line, 5.56 mm NATO manglers tumbling and fragmenting as they penetrated solid flesh. The bullets were designed to cause massive internal injuries—*cavitation*, in clinical lingo—and drop a target in his tracks. Bolan had seen the gross effects in training films and in the flesh.

Like now.

Garcelle had covered half the distance to her fallen pistol, favoring her right wrist as she crawled across the sidewalk. Wild rounds from one of her father's flunkies cracked concrete in front of her, and while she flinched, she also kept going.

Take her now? Or wait until she reached the gun?

The new front-runner for the Haitian skirmish line had almost cleared the sidewalk's grassy verge, rounding the bench Garcelle had occupied until a moment earlier. He stopped there, dropping to one knee and lining up his shot, an elbow on top of the bench's armrest to provide stability.

Too late.

Bolan already had him lined up in the Steyr's telescopic sight, stroking the rifle's trigger, blowing him away. He thought the dead man had a vaguely stunned expression on his face, something the Executioner had seen before.

And something he would see again.

ABNER BIASSOU HAD BEEN ordered not to interfere while Garcelle killed the white man, to intervene only if she failed. He'd been watching when she drew her pistol and the stranger easily disarmed her, seemed about to take her hostage—or at least interrogate her—when he knew it was time to move.

"Close in!" he commanded, leaping to his feet and wobbling for a heartbeat, then finding his stride. He heard the others running, some already closer to the target than Biassou was. He saw the white man shove Garcelle, knocking her down, and barked another order through his Bluetooth headset.

"Kill him! But be careful of the girl!"

One of his men—he thought it might be Janjak—fired a short burst at the enemy and missed. The white man wasted no time in returning fire, taking Biassou's soldier down.

"Damn!"

Biassou raised his weapon, an M4 carbine fitted with a vertical foregrip and an Aimpoint CompM2 sight. He tried to aim while running, but everything was a blur, with the red dot dancing like a cat toy's laser beam.

He lurched to a halt, saw a second member of his ambush party falling to his left, and took a moment to line up his shot. The white man had hunched down, was moving, making it more difficult, but Abner reckoned he could do this, get full credit for it, and perhaps reap some reward.

Another second, now. His index finger curled around the carbine's trigger, taking up the slack, his right eye peering through the CompM2's reticle. He saw the red dot waver, then lock tight onto the white man's chest. The sight did not emit a laser beam, so his target was unaware, dropping a third man, oblivious to Death approaching.

Biassou squeezed the M4's trigger—and felt his heart stop as Garcelle leaped from the sidewalk, lurching up into his line of fire, pistol in hand. His bullets cut into her from behind, making her stumble, spin around. There was time for her to blink at him, astounded, just before she fell.

Biassou felt the scream rising inside him, ripping from his throat before he could contain it. As she dropped, he knew his life was over, could imagine how her father would react, exacting vengeance by the slow and agonizing hour, likely days on end, until Biassou prayed for death and met it as a blessing.

Howling like a berserker in the night, he charged the white man. Incoherent, barely conscious, he barked orders, curses, insults to his soldiers through the Bluetooth headset, firing from the hip with his M4. He wished the rifle's magazine had tracers in it, so he could watch the bullets strike his target, maybe set the man afire, but all he saw was agile movement, his intended victim rolling to one side and popping up again, his weapon sighting on Biassou.

When the bullets struck him, spalling on impact with his ribs and sternum, fragments shearing through his heart, lungs, liver, stomach, it was almost a relief. Biassou tripped over his own feet, fell into the darkness waiting for him and was gone.

BOLAN HAD NO TIME to consider Garcelle dying on the sidewalk, almost at his feet. The man who'd cut her down was charging at him, firing, wailing like a wounded animal, and he had only seconds to hit him with another of the Steyr's muffled bursts, dropping his corpse almost atop the woman's.

Four more enemies still in the game, and they were closing on him now, after a moment's hesitation when Garcelle was shot. Not something they'd expected, obviously, but they had to make the best of it, couldn't go back to Jean Brouard saying they'd lost his daughter *and* the man she'd come to kill. For them, survival hinged on taking Bolan down, and they were giving it their best shots, literally, automatic weapons chattering.

He couldn't run, had no cover to speak of, so he dropped and rolled. Bullets hummed through the air above him like a swarm of insects pumped on steroids, poorly aimed in the excitement and confusion of the moment, but still lethal. Bolan fired, rolled, fired and rolled again, trusting his instincts and the AUG's Swarovski Optik to put his rounds on target.

The nearest shooter ran into a triple-tap of 5.56 mm shockers. Dying on his feet and vaulting backward through a clumsy sort of somersault, he was left twisted on the pavement, facing back the way he'd come, quivering in time with the blood pulsing from his fatal wounds.

The next Haitian in line witnessed his comrade falling, ducked and sidestepped in a hasty reflex action, but it couldn't save him. Bolan took him with a rising burst, the first round drilling him above the navel, two and three striking his solar plexus and his throat, respectively. The world's best body armor would not have protected him, and he was wearing none. No two men die exactly the same way, however, and this soldier toppled forward, kissed the sidewalk with a crack of breaking teeth and cartilage, his weapon trapped and stuttering beneath him, sending bullets east along the sidewalk.

Doing part of Bolan's job, as it turned out. The stray slugs hacked through a man's legs before he had a chance to duck or dodge. The wounded Haitian screamed, went down as if someone had yanked a rug from under him, but clearly wasn't finished yet.

Another burst from Bolan's AUG accomplished that, cutting the wounded soldier's face to shreds and shattering his skull. The headless Haitian toppled over backward, arms flung out as if preparing for a crucifixion, bleeding out from both ends.

Only one remained, and he was hesitating now, aware that he'd been left alone to face the man his team had marked down as an easy kill. He hissed at Bolan, turned as if to flee, and managed two long strides before a silent burst slapped home between his shoulder blades, giving him wings for all the time it took to execute a nosedive, tumbling on the grassy verge.

Sirens.

Bolan was out of time and he knew it, rising from the pavement, turning back toward Town Park and the Mercury Marauder waiting for him there. He left nine bodies scattered on the grass and sidewalk, dark blood pooling, forming abstract patterns as it spread. Police would send the message home to Jean Brouard, and Bolan thought he just might leave it there. Not out of any sympathy for him or for Garcelle, but to concentrate on why he'd traveled to Miami in the first place.

It was time to finish with the Viper Posse there, and then move on.

6

Liberty City, Miami

Winston Channer listened to the news report and wondered what to make of it. His men were not the ones who'd been killed, this time, and while that pleased him, still he was confused. The blonde on his television screen said eight men had been killed at Williams Park, along with a woman identified as Garcelle Brouard, daughter of "a reputed Haitian mobster."

What in hell was happening?

On one hand, Channer was relieved. When it got back to Kingston, Quarrie might believe he was responsible and give him credit for rebounding from his wounds and settling one score, at least. It could make matters worse, if he found out the truth, but who would tell him?

An idea struck Channer and made his stomach churn. What if Quarrie himself had done this thing? There'd been ample time for posse reinforcements to reach Miami—just under two hours in actual flight time from Kingston—but how could Quarrie have arranged the ambush? He was clever, certainly—and some said magical—but even with Obeah working for him, was it possible?

Channer thought not, which left the problem he'd started with.

Who was responsible, and why?

He'd thought of leaving, simply bailing out and running for his life, but that idea stalled out when he considered destinations. Anyplace on Earth with a Jamaican population left him vulnerable to the Viper Posse; on the other hand, if there were no Jamaicans in the spot he chose, he would stand out and draw attention to himself, bringing the hunters down upon him.

And there could be no mistake: Quarrie would track him down, intent on vengeance, if he ran.

What, then? The walls of his ghetto hideout felt as if they were closing around him, and the ganja was not helping.

Well, not much. He lit another spliff and drew the smoke into his lungs, hoping he could relax a little, at the very least. Being a target was hard work, and all the worse when Channer could not say exactly who was stalking him.

Brouard would want his Rasta scalp, of course, but it was obvious the Haitian had not killed his own soldiers, much less his daughter. That sounded like Quarrie, and yet....

Channer thought of the white man, and that confused him even more. Why would the stranger pluck Garcelle Brouard from Channer's clutches, just to kill her hours later? Something strange was at work here, and his poor brain, fogged by pain and drugs, could not make out the details.

Rum might help.

He'd already killed the best part of a brand-new bottle, but his tolerance was high these days. He barely wobbled on his feet while crossing to the liquor cabinet, filling a glass and walking back to settle on the sofa. He had submachine guns lined up on the coffee table at his knee—two Uzis and an MP5, all cocked and locked—together with a pair of pistols and a switchblade with a polished ebony handle. His men were standing guard in shifts, inside the house and outside, prepared to sacrifice themselves in his defense.

Now what?

He smoked and drank, turned on the television set once more and started flipping through channels. Nothing he saw amused him. Channer needed *action*, some means of proving himself *to* himself—and to Quarrie in Kingston. An opportunity to make things right and lift the pall of failure that had settled over him.

He found a cop show on TV, some kind of SWAT team battling a gang not very different from his own. The shooting soothed him, brutal scenes requiring no analysis of any kind. Seconds later, when one of the officers from Babylon set off a stun grenade, the windows of his own house rattled.

What the—?

Channer bolted to his feet, dropping his nearly empty glass and scooping up one of the Uzis. He could hear his soldiers shouting, smelled the smoke of ordnance, realizing in a heartbeat that the blast had not been on TV.

Trembling, he went to seek redemption with the Uzi clutched against his chest.

FINDING CHANNER'S HIDEOUT hadn't proved as difficult as Bolan had expected. He'd snatched one of the Viper Posse's stragglers from a club in Kendall, squeezed him till his courage snapped and filed the address in his head. Liberty City was predominately black, but had enough whites and Hispanics salted through the mix to let him move with confidence along its streets. The hour helped, as well. Most of the district's people were home in bed, regardless of profession or their standing with the law.

Even the predators need sleep.

He found the house and made a drive-by recon, spotting two men on the stoop. They had no weapons showing but he knew there would be hardware within easy reach. Bolan considered stopping at the curb, out front, and wasting them before he rushed the house, but then decided to employ a bit more subtlety.

Not much, but just enough.

He parked down range and took the Barrett sniper rifle from its place on the Marauder's broad backseat. He screwed a bulky silencer onto its muzzle, knowing its efficiency was compromised by the .338 Lapua Magnum ammo's muzzle velocity, but it would still muffle the shots and buy some time for him to close the distance from his auto to the target house on foot.

Slinging the Steyr from his shoulder, Bolan peered through the rifle's telescopic sight and found his first mark lounging underneath a yellow porch light chosen to repel mosquitoes. He timed his shot, working the bolt action in his mind before his index finger curled around the trigger, taking up the slack.

He squeezed and rode the big gun's recoil, didn't bother watching as his target's skull exploded, shifting toward the second while the bolt slid smoothly, out and back. A second round reached out to tag the other goon, making a *crack* in midflight as it broke Mach 3. He stowed the piece before his secondary target finished thrashing on the porch and locked the car behind him, sprinting toward the house Channer had chosen as his hideaway.

Before he hit the sidewalk, starting up a grassy pathway to the house, Bolan had palmed a frag grenade and pulled its pin, pitching the green egg through a window facing the street and crouching while he counted down the short life of its fuse. On detonation, he was up and moving while the M68's shrapnel ripped into flesh, walls and furniture inside the house. At the door, he kicked through and burst in with his rifle leading, to a parlor that had turned into a slaughterhouse.

A dead man was on the sofa, head down, dreadlocks dangling, blank eyes staring at the blood pool in his lap. Not far away, a second Viper Posse goon was wriggling on the carpet, pushing with his elbows, dragging shattered legs behind him, leaving rusty-colored tracks. Bolan couldn't understand what he was saying to himself, a steady muttering, and didn't try to work it out, just tagged him with a mercy round behind one ear and finished it.

It was a start, but only that. Until he'd dealt with Winston Channer, Bolan's labors in Miami were not done.

LINTON FRASER KNEW his place, and that was watching over Winston Channer. The odds were good that he would die along with Channer, cut down at the tender age of twenty-three.

No matter. He'd been *born dead*—the Viper Posse's motto—one of thousands in Jamaica who'd faced a hopeless life of poverty until he'd been discovered by the men who made him special, someone admired by the younger street urchins of Tivoli Gardens in Kingston. Preachers might decry his lifestyle, but he wasn't hungry anymore, and never would be in his life again.

However short that was.

"We need to go now, Boss," he said, and got a nod from Channer in return. The boss man reeked of ganja, which was normal, and of spiced rum. He was on his feet, though, fairly steady, and he seemed to have a firm grip on the Uzi SMG.

"Out through the back," Fraser suggested, since the front had obviously gone to hell with the explosion, gunfire and his fellow soldiers shouting. Fraser didn't know who was attacking them—police, the Haitians, someone else—and at the moment, it was of no interest to him. Getting Winston Channer clear of danger was the only thing that mattered.

You could say his life depended on it.

"Did you see a white man?" Channer asked.

White man? Fraser had no idea what his boss was talking about. "No, sir," he answered. "Come with me, now."

"If he's here, I'm gonna kill him," Channer said.

"Maybe tomorrow," Fraser suggested, as more gunfire rang through the house. "The brothers are dealin' it now."

"All right," Channer agreed at last. Fraser began to lead him toward the back door, hoping they weren't too late already. Even as they passed into the hallway, bullets ripped through drywall close behind them, spraying chalky dust.

Too close for comfort.

If they escaped from the house, they had a choice of exiting the neighborhood on foot, or using one of the cars parked on a nearby lot, fenced in and under guard to keep the local thugs from stealing them or vandalizing them.

Driving was better, safer, but it suddenly occurred to Fraser that he didn't have keys to any of the posse vehicles. For that matter, he couldn't even clear the padlocked gate that foiled casual trespassers, and agile as he was, he didn't fancy scaling the fence with its coil of razor wire on top.

"Wait, Boss," he said. "You have the car keys?"

"Why'n hell would I?" Channer demanded.

"I'll go find them," Fraser said. "You stay here."

Channer responded with a wobbly nod. "Don't drag your ass," he added. "Hurry!"

Fraser almost had to laugh at that. As if he'd dawdle. As if both of them weren't running for their lives.

He knew exactly where the keys were kept, inside an ornate little cabinet, nailed to the kitchen wall. That meant heading toward the sounds of battle, not something he relished, but he had no choice.

Get on with it.

Cursing under his breath, he ran back toward the fight.

AFTER THE SECOND FRAG grenade went off, Bolan rose from the cover of an upturned dining table and surveyed his fallen enemies. There had been four of them, and all were down, though not entirely out.

One man was obviously dead, his face reduced to something the consistency of hamburger, one arm almost detached from its shoulder. Another, lying close by, seemed to be gurgling his last breaths through holes in his chest. The other two, by contrast, might have some fight left in them. One was whimpering, a red hand covering a shrapnel wound in his left thigh, but he was straining for the TEC-9 he had dropped when the explosion knocked him sprawling. Farther off to Bolan's right, a gunman scalped by flying steel was on his knees, shaking his head, still clinging to the MAC-10 he'd been holding when it all went down.

Bolan dealt with the kneeling gunner first, drilling his bloodied forehead with a 5.56 mm round that slapped him over backward, dropping with his legs folded beneath him in a posture that would certainly have spiked his knees with pain, if he'd still been alive. A problem he would never have again.

The soldier with the wounded leg was cursing, scrabbling for his weapon, but it lay beyond his reach. Bolan had no time to play games with him, just hit him with another single shot that silenced him for good. The other two were no concern of his, so he moved on.

Beyond the room where he'd taken out the four defenders, Bolan heard more shouting, cursing, scrambling, as surviving members of the home team rallied to repel the invaders. Most of them were brave enough, their courage likely boosted by a mix of ganja and religious fervor, but it wasn't helping them so far. Still, their response— wild fire with automatic weapons, and to hell with consequences—posed a threat to Bolan as he moved deeper into their lair.

He was looking for Winston Channer, hoping to find him before he slipped away. Bolan's time in Liberty City was running short. Police were bound to turn up soon, and a shooting call from the ghetto would bring uniforms out in force.

Bolan ducked into the kitchen, where he found a solitary Rasta soldier sorting through a rack of keys inside a wooden cabinet. The shooter caught a flicker of motion in his peripheral vision, spinning to face his opponent. Keys rattled onto the floor around his feet, as he blurted, "You're in big trouble, comin' here. You're gonna die!"

He'd tucked a pistol into his waistband while he fiddled with the keys. Now he tried to draw it in the face of sudden death but Bolan's double-tap got there ahead of him. His target squeezed off a shot by reflex with the muzzle of his handgun still tucked in his pants, a splash of blood he likely never felt staining the fabric at his fly. He dropped, half sitting with his back against the wall below the cabinet, keys spread around his legs.

Evacuating on his own, or with somebody else?

Bolan checked on the AUG's translucent magazine, and went back to the hunt.

Two minutes later, Channer guessed that Fraser wasn't coming back. It was a thirty-second walk to the kitchen, less than half that running, and he clearly should have returned with the keys by now.

So he was dead or dying. Channer's only hope now was to take his Uzi and depart on foot, run as fast and as far as he could without meeting the invaders or stumbling over police. Liberty City was a ghetto, granted, but one of his neighbors was bound to call Babylon, what with the volume of fire coming out of the house.

It was enough to wake the dead, or maybe put them down again.

Where would he go? No matter. Getting out was all that counted, at the moment.

And he had to start *right now*.

"I'm outta here," he muttered to himself, and turned toward the back door.

Before he moved, though, legs still rubbery from too much rum and ganja, Channer heard the gunfire from a nearby room increase in volume and intensity. The enemy—whoever *he* was—must have met his last line of defense. That line was holding, by the sound of it, but might not do for long.

When the explosion came, it was as loud as thunder to his ringing ears. Channer dropped to one knee, his wounded arm reaching out instinctively to find a wall and lancing him with pain, while his left hand clutched the Uzi. It felt heavier than usual, as if his strength was starting to desert him by degrees.

A cloud of smoke and dust rolled toward him from the room where Channer's men were dying. All for what? To keep him safe? And there he was, unfit even to stand and run away.

Smoke stung his eyes and tried to choke him. Channer was struggling to his feet when he saw something—some*one*—moving in the haze before him. He was tall, no features visible as yet, impossible to say if he was friend or foe.

"Who's that?" he demanded, barely croaking out the words.

No reply from the smoke.

"Somebody better answer me!" he barked.

In spite of all he'd seen and heard that night, the shot was a surprise. It struck his left shoulder, ripped through the ball-and-socket joint, spinning Channer ninety degrees to his left as he fell—and landed, naturally—on the right arm. He nearly passed out then, but bit his lip to keep a fragile grip on consciousness as he lay trembling on the floor.

Waiting to die.

It was the only end he could envision—no mercy from his enemy. If their positions were reversed, Channer would kill his adversary without thinking twice, unless he had an opportunity to question him before the end. In this case, clearly, there was no time for interrogation.

So, all his hopes and aspirations finally came down to nothing.

A shadow fell across his face, and Channer stared up at his executioner.

"WHAT'S YOUR NAME?" Channer asked.

"Not important," Bolan said, denying him even that much.

"You gonna kill me?"

"Any reason why I shouldn't?"

"None I can think of."

"Well, then."

Numbers falling in his head. Time running out.

"Who sent you after me?"

"Enough talk," Bolan said, and put a NATO round through Channer's left eye at a range of six feet, tops. Impact distorted his pain-twisted features into something like a fright mask, while a slick of blood began to spread beneath his shattered skull.

Over and out.

Bolan went out the back door, circling around behind the house and back toward Northwest 62nd Street. The Marauder sat where he'd left it, unmolested, although there were people on the street now, craning for a look at Channer's house. Some of them gaped at Bolan as he sprinted past, mostly looking at his weapons, but they didn't try to stop him.

Wise decision.

He assumed someone would describe his ride to the police when they arrived, maybe recall his license number, or at least a fragment of it. None of that was his concern. He had a drop planned for the car, and by the time he ditched it, he'd be on his way to Miami International. Sometime within the next few hours, he'd be airborne, on his way to Kingston and the next phase of his mission.

Given time and opportunity, he would have liked to pay a call on Jean Brouard, arrange a father-and-child reunion, but that was off the table for the moment. He would file the Haitian's name away, remember him, and possibly return to settle that account another time.

Sitting in the airport's long-term parking lot, he placed a call to Stony Man and told whoever answered where the Mercury could be retrieved. If cops arrived before the pickup driver came, so be it. Either way, the arsenal locked in its trunk would be secure, not lifted to supply a local street gang. Bolan left his parking ticket in the glove compartment, with the keys, and locked the driver's door behind him as he went to catch the airport's shuttle bus.

He'd made it through Miami one more time, leaving his enemies in disarray. Feds and police could do the mopping up, and maybe build some decent cases from the wreckage Bolan left behind. He had another job to do, meanwhile.

It was waiting for him in Jamaica, and the worst was still to come.

7

Windward Road, Kingston, Jamaica

"When they get here, we'll be ready for them."

"When who gets here?" Trevor Seaga asked.

"Whoever's comin', brother," Jerome Quarrie said. "You don't think the trouble in Miami's a coincidence? They'll be here soon."

"But who?"

"Winston said it's one bad boy, but he couldn't stop 'em. Now he's dead. We won't make the same mistake."

"I got the brothers ready. We won't have any trouble here."

"We'd better not," Quarrie advised him.

He was troubled, all the same. Miami was—had been—his gateway into the United States, his richest market. New York, with its teeming millions, had been resisting strong incursions by the Viper Posse. It would take time to rebuild the operation in Miami, if it could be done at all. Police of every stripe were swarming through the city, hunting Quarrie's men who'd managed to survive the firestorm.

Not too many, if he understood the last reports correctly.

At first, he'd suspected Haitians. Winston Channer had been tussling with Jean Brouard. Still, the news from Florida and Channer's own reports failed to support that notion. Channer had been up against a white man, maybe more than one, and while Brouard could certainly afford to hire an assassin—or an army of them, for that matter—it wasn't his style.

So, someone else. But who?

The killings in Miami didn't seem official. Quarrie knew how devious the ways of Babylon could be, had taken full advantage of them in his rise to power, but the beast had rules. Given a choice, Miami officers, the FBI or DEA, whatever, would prefer to operate within the framework of their laws. Get warrants from a court before they staged raids, ransacked homes and offices, killed people with the television crews recording it. They wanted glory to justify their swollen budgets, and they couldn't have it if they posed as gangsters running wild.

That brought him back to *someone else*, which left him nowhere.

Whoever it was, they'd soon find a world of difference between pushing Quarrie's men around in Florida and trying it in Kingston. This was *his* town.

"I don't want no one sleepin' on the job," Quarrie told his second in command. "Somebody drops the ball, he answers to me personally."

"The brothers know that."

"You make *sure* they know it. That's your job."

"When have I ever failed you?" Trevor asked.

"First time for anything," Quarrie replied. "And the first time is the last."

Norman Manley International Airport, Palisadoes, Jamaica

BOLAN'S AIR JAMAICA FLIGHT landed a few ticks shy of noon. The next half hour was consumed by taxiing, parking the 737 jetliner and getting all its passengers prepared to exit from the plane in single file. Outside, the day's heat and humidity settled on Bolan like a thick, wet blanket.

He passed through customs without incident, his "Matthew Cooper" passport raising no suspicion from the bored agent who asked his business in Jamaica, took "tourism" as a satisfactory response, and stamped a page at random. Visas weren't required for American visitors unless they planned to hang around the island longer than six months. That made it easy, since his mission— if it went as planned—would be measured in hours or, at most, days.

He'd booked a ride from a car rental inside the airport terminal, and found the young, attractive agent helpful to a fault. She photocopied Matthew Cooper's United States driver's license, swiped his credit card and recommended full insurance coverage, which Bolan accepted. When that was done, she handed him the keys to a Toyota Camry, a wide-body four-door sedan with sufficient trunk space for a body or two. The car was silver, pretty much the same as gray, and wouldn't stand out in a crowd—at least, until its 3.5-liter V6 engine kicked in.

Bolan left the airport and drove into Kingston proper, a city that was seething with crime. Travel advisories from the US State Department spelled it out in no uncertain terms: random gunfire in the streets, drug trafficking, armed robberies of tourists, sexual assaults by staffers at the city's vacation resorts.

But today, Jamaica and its bad boys were about to get a rude surprise.

Their nemesis was coming.

Embassy of the United States, Kingston

DALE HOLBROOK WAS a go-to guy. A fixer, problem solver, pick your label. When he'd done his bit in the Marine

Corps, he'd been a scrounger for his company, producing treasured items on demand. These past five years, he'd been a wunderkind of sorts for the Central Intelligence Agency.

And now, Langley had dumped a steaming load of bullshit on his plate.

The call had come in shortly after 6:00 a.m. on the scrambled line, the second deputy director of the National Clandestine Service, Regional and Transnational Issues Division. The guy's name was Stark, and it fit like a lead-weighted glove.

"We've got a problem," Stark had told him. Meaning *Holbrook* had a problem, since shit always ran downhill. "Jamaicans."

"What about them?" he'd inquired.

"They're getting killed in Miami, and we think the trouble's headed your way."

Holbrook had to scowl at that, the sour taste already in his mouth. He didn't need to hear the rest of it, but Stark went on anyway.

It was, of course, the Viper Posse. Outwardly, the syndicate was nothing but a bunch of lowlife narco traffickers and thrill-killers. Given a choice, Holbrook would not have dealt with them at any price, but when you were a go-to guy for Langley, choice evaporated.

The bottom line in Kingston: criminal posses were inextricably linked to both the People's National Party and its primary rival, Jamaica Labour Party. The gangs smuggled drugs and weapons, two commodities that brought them into contact with a murky world of terrorists, conspirators and dirty politicians.

So many secrets, waiting to be coaxed or purchased from the posses, in exchange for turning blind eyes toward their dirty deals Stateside. It was a classic bargain for the Agency, which had been cuddling up to criminals since its creation, in the Cold War era. The cartels were a gold mine, both of covert information and clandestine cash that bankrolled operations off the books, unsupervised by Washington.

So, sure, the vital link must be maintained. And anyone who tried to sever it must be identified, then crushed like an insect. Holbrook had done similar errands before, most recently in Afghanistan, and he knew the drill by heart.

One catch: Stark didn't have a clue who they were dealing with this time.

"So, what am I supposed to do with that?" he'd asked his boss.

"Whatever's necessary," Stark had answered. "Get it done. That's all."

"No matter what?"

"You really need to ask?"

Not really, no. It was a rhetorical question, and wasted on the second deputy director of the NCS-RTID. As usual, results were all that mattered.

First step: contact the Viper Posse's leader, cautiously, and learn about the mess in Florida. Offer the Agency's assistance—strictly unofficially, of course—in making sure the problem didn't spread to Kingston next. If Quarrie wouldn't play, Holbrook had other contacts in the capital, including several highly placed officers of the Jamaica Constabulary Force, working both Narcotics and on the Organized Crime and Anti-Corruption Task Force. They'd help him if they could…at a price.

Way of the world.

Holbrook was blessed—or cursed—with an eidetic memory. He never wrote down any information that could turn around and bite him later, whether it be names, addresses, phone numbers, or details of some criminal conspiracy in which he was involved. It was a matter of survival, and he lost no sleep over the things he'd done or ordered to be done.

As far as Holbrook was concerned, the CIA was a sanctioned criminal conspiracy, unleashed to roam the world and violate the laws of other nations. Since the shock of 9/11, it also enjoyed a virtual carte blanche on the home front.

And why not?

What really mattered, after all, besides the USA, its wants and needs? The world at large was just a pasture where fat American livestock grazed at will, reaping the best of everything.

Ready for the challenge he'd been given, Holbrook pressed the scrambler button on his private line and started making calls.

Greenwich Town, Kingston, Jamaica

THE DEALER RAN a pawn shop on 4th Street, two blocks north of Marcus Garvey Drive. Bolan had acquired the man's name and address via Stony Man. He hadn't called ahead, in case the pawnbroker—one Simon Reid, proprietor of Kingston Loans—decided it would profit him to rat a stranger out to the police. Once Bolan had acquired the gear he needed, paying with untraceable cash, Reid could file reports with whomever he liked.

At his own risk, of course.

The shop was small, squeezed in between a beauty parlor and a storefront law office. No other customers were around when Bolan parked his Camry on the street out front, locked it and went inside. Reid was a slender sixty-something man with salt-and-pepper hair, mirrored by a goatee that could have used a trim. His smile flashed gold; his handshake was a modest squeeze, quickly withdrawn.

Bolan explained his business, spoke a name Stony Man

had given him to prove his bona fides, watching as the golden smile dimmed slightly. Dealing with a stranger in the arms trade was a risky proposition for both sides, and Reid was understandably cautious. Still, greed won out when Bolan mentioned figures, and he locked the shop's front door, turning its OPEN sign around to indicate the place was CLOSED.

The basement arsenal was roughly half the size of Kingston Loans's upstairs. The space was air-conditioned and climate controlled, fighting the endless tropical war against rust and corrosion. The weapons racked along three walls looked new, well tended, worth their weight in gold to anyone in a hurry, dodging the Jamaican Firearms Act and its registration fee.

Reid guided "Matthew Cooper" on a tour of his inventory: assault rifles, submachine guns, shotguns, pistols and various specialty items, quoting prices as they went. Bolan's first choice was an L85A1 assault rifle, a dependable bullpup design chambered in 5.56 mm NATO. The British rifle came with a SUSAT 4x telescopic sight— short for Sight Unit Small Arms Trilux—that included tritium-powered illumination for shooting in the gray hours of dawn and dusk.

Next up, he chose a Glock 18 pistol, the selective-fire version of Glock's original sidearm chambered in 9 mm Parabellum, capable of firing semi- or full-auto at the flip of a switch. Reid stocked Glock magazines holding seventeen and thirty-three rounds, prompting Bolan to pick up a dozen of each.

For long-distance work, just in case, he went British again, selecting an AS50 sniper/anti-materiel rifle from Accuracy International. Chambered for .50-caliber Browning Machine Gun rounds, in skilled hands it could fire off five in less than two seconds, killing out to eighteen hundred meters with dependable consistency.

Bolan completed his shopping with military webbing, a fast-draw shoulder rig for the Glock 18, spare magazines and ammo all around, and a dozen British L109A1 HE fragmentation grenades filled with RDX, featuring a fuse delay of three to four seconds. On a whim, he added a Chaos trench knife from Cold Steel, featuring a 7.5-inch double-edged carbon steel blade and an aluminum grip with D-ring knuckle-dusters, and a stud on the pommel for shattering skulls. He donned the shoulder holster, packed the rest into duffel bags and paid his bill with cash donated by Channer's posse in Miami, leaving Simon Reid with smiles, handshakes and the implicit knowledge that betrayal rated death.

Back on the street at last, the hunt began.

Tivoli Gardens, Kingston

JEROME QUARRIE WAS SEEKING aid and comfort from the Other Side. His first resort in any crisis was personal strength and firepower, but as a child of the islands he also liked to hedge his bets. Obeah had been useful in the past, and might be again, now that he faced an unknown enemy.

Quarrie stopped short of publicly declaring belief in supernatural realms. He prided himself on being a modern Jamaican, on working the system—but there were systems and *systems* in twenty-first-century Kingston. He'd seen firsthand the power and influence Obeah held over some of his superstitious countrymen, and he'd taken full advantage of it in the past, to cow opponents, witnesses and people who possessed something he desired.

Besides, what could it hurt—except, of course, the object of his latest sacrifice.

The ritual den stood on Rum Stores Road, near Kingston's waterfront. Quarrie arrived in his Lincoln MKS limousine, with only his driver and one guard. Neither

entered the den with their boss, since the rite he planned
to perform was for his eyes only. Inside, two distinctly
different men had prepared the scene.

The first, well-known to Quarrie, was Usain Dalhouse,
an Obeah priest, or *papaloi*. He might have been fifty
years old or one hundred; Quarrie found it pointless to
guess. The priest had weathered skin, and he was clean-
shaven from scalp to waist. Dalhouse had removed his
shirt, as usual, to show a chest adorned with swirling
red and green tattoos. His pants were blue jeans cut off
at the knees, faded from countless washings that hadn't
eradicated all of their peculiar, rust-colored stains, and
he stood barefoot on the concrete floor.

Quarrie had never seen the other man before. He was a
cipher, name unknown and of no interest. Much younger
than the *papaloi*, perhaps in his early twenties, he lay nude
on a gurney that stood with its wheels locked, becoming a
makeshift altar. Padded straps restrained the young man's
arms and legs, but he wasn't tugging against them. Dark
eyes, fully open, stared with rapt attention at the ceiling
and fluorescent fixtures overhead.

Sedated on the last day of his life.

As usual, the *papaloi* had already prepared the sacrifice, painting arcane symbols in white on the man's dark
chest and abdomen, across his forehead and around his
eyes. A small stainless-steel table on casters stood beside the gurney, draped with a towel. Atop the towel lay
a single object: an *athame*, or ritual dagger, silver handle
and guard fashioned to resemble writhing serpents, its
curved fifteen-inch blade inscribed with symbols of oc-
cult significance. From prior experience, Quarrie knew
that its cutting edge was razor sharp.

"Prepare yourself," the ageless *papaloi* commanded.

Obeying silently, Quarrie removed his jacket, tie and
shirt, then finally his shoes, trousers and stockings. The

breeze from a swamp cooler briefly chilled him. Standing next to naked in designer underwear, he approached the altar.

Rituals had to be performed before he did his part. A prayer for strength and the destruction of his enemies took roughly fifteen minutes, Quarrie standing with his head bowed, eyes closed, echoing the *papaloi*'s words as the old man circled around him, blowing smoke from a cigar and spitting rum over the supine sacrifice. When he was done, the *papaloi* stood back and said, "Proceed."

Quarrie picked up the *athame*. The trick, he knew, was getting to the heart and clutching it before it stopped beating. If he could manage that—or, better yet, hold it aloft with blood still pumping from its severed arteries—his entreaties stood a better chance of being granted.

Was it all a foolish waste of time?

Lifting the heavy dagger, Quarrie realized he didn't care.

8

Trench Town, Kingston, Jamaica

Bolan rolled past a chipped and faded sign that read "Welcome to Trench Town the Home of Reggae Music," and passed into another world. He'd already grown accustomed to the signs of poverty in Kingston, but the neighborhood surrounding him as dusk crept over the capital city was nothing short of bizarre.

Everywhere he looked, through windows streaked with drizzling rain, he faced colorful murals depicting Haile Selassie or reggae musician Bob Marley. Sometimes the two were side by side, with Marley toking on a ganja blunt. Some murals added Marley's son Ziggy, beaming smiles that might be taken as a welcome or a challenge. Interspersed with the dramatic art were countless run-down shops—some at the point of collapse—people ambling past food stalls, rusty cars, graffiti with the usual obscure messages: "Exodus," "Rise!" and "Telaviv Dread."

The Executioner was en route to Arnett Gardens, a Trench Town housing project known to locals as "The Jungle." Within the sprawling complex was a Viper Posse nest whose members peddled drugs, extorted money from the project's tenants and surrounding shops, enforced their own rough "justice" on the streets, and generally made life miserable in the neighborhood.

Bolan knew where to find them.

Getting in and out would be the trick.

First thing, he didn't try to hide his rental car. Bolan parked at the curb and waited for the teenagers to come, drawn like iron filings to a magnet. When he had a dozen standing by, he stepped out of the car and asked, "How much for you to watch my ride?"

Their spokesman smiled and asked, "How much you carrying?"

Bolan produced a roll of currency and fanned it out, left-handed, showing it around to startled eyes. "Is this enough?"

"Do you have more?" another of them asked.

"I do," Bolan replied, lifting the L85A1 into view with his right hand. "We good?"

"Your car'll be here when you get back," their leader said.

"In one piece," Bolan said, not asking them.

"Sure, man. No worries."

Bolan handed the leader his roll, some of Winston Channer's money, and left them to share it out. As he approached The Jungle, he removed a ski mask from another pocket, tugging it over his head. Not worried much about a witness coming forward to describe him to police, he chose to work the psywar angle where he could.

Inside, the place was filthy, reeking, tagged with graffiti on every available wall. He chose a flight of stairs and climbed it to the second floor, surprising tenants who were lounging in the corridor. They scattered, ducking into nearby apartments, some edging around him and fleeing when Bolan passed.

As he approached the posse's lair, a lookout saw him coming, shouted through the open door, and reached for something under his baggy T-shirt, depicting a lion with dreadlocks. Bolan didn't give him time to draw whatever weapon he was after, triggering a 3-round burst that drilled the silk-screened lion through its forehead, opening the lookout's chest and blowing him away.

It hit the fan then, posse soldiers spilling from the flat like hornets from a ruptured hive, all armed and shouting curses, threats, whatever, as they opened fire. Bolan dropped underneath their first rounds, going prone, and raked the milling skirmish line with 5.56 mm manglers, shredding flesh and fabric, spraying blood in abstract patterns on the dingy walls, brass tinkling on the concrete floor.

A moment later, everything was still, except for babies wailing somewhere in the distance, sad cries muffled by The Jungle's walls. He rose and moved among the leaking dead, peered into their apartment, checking for survivors, finding none.

Reloading as he left the flat, Bolan retraced his path out of The Jungle. People watched him pass from doorways, here and there, then hastily withdrew like turtles ducking back into their shells. Outside, full dark was settling over Arnett Gardens as he walked back to his car.

Still there, in good shape, with its guardians on duty. Watching Bolan with a kind of awe as he stripped off his ski mask, tucked it out of sight and tossed another bankroll to their leader.

"Job well-done," he said.

The kid smiled back at Bolan, gave a little bow and said, "Come back anytime!"

Downtown Kingston

THE RESTAURANT STOOD on Hanover Street, two blocks south of East Queen. Dale Holbrook was early, seated alone in a booth with his back to the wall, waiting for Quarrie to make his grand entrance. The Viper

Posse's boss loved drama as much as he loved easy cash. Maybe more.

Holbrook had ordered coffee on arrival, sipped it slowly, savoring the Jamaican Blue Mountain flavor that sold Stateside for forty-odd dollars a pound. Unlike some other people he could name, the caffeine made him mellow, put his mind and nerves at ease.

Which he could use, right now.

Meeting Quarrie in public was dicey, a risk at best, career suicide at worst. They hadn't been caught yet, and Holbrook only set such meetings in the direst of emergencies. Unfortunately, this was one of those—or could turn into one, unless he nipped their problem in the bud.

For that, he needed Quarrie's help.

Five minutes later, Quarrie strolled in behind a pair of burly bodyguards, with two more trailing in his wake. The shooters peeled away to find their places, two at the counter, two more in a booth near the door, as Quarrie made his way to Holbrook's table. Holbrook rose, nodded, then sat again when Quarrie did.

"You have a worried face," he said.

"I've been advised about your difficulties in Miami," Holbrook said. "Instructed to cooperate and make the problem go away."

"Instructed. Not your choice, then."

Holbrook held the gangster's level gaze. "I get assignments and complete them. We've been working well together so far. No one wants to see that partnership disrupted."

"I think somebody does," Quarrie replied. "He's been killin' my brothers all over South Florida."

"My people weren't aware of that before it happened," Holbrook said. "It didn't come from us, I promise you."

"Who, then? Some other part of the alphabet? The FBI or DEA? Homeland Obscurity?"

"We're working on it energetically. No answers yet."

"What good are you to me, then?" Quarrie asked him.

"I have contacts, resources. If this guy's from the States, I have a longer reach than you do."

"And when you find him?"

"Your call. I can either hand him over or dispose of him myself."

"Kill him yourself? I'd like to see that." Quarrie laughed.

"Whatever it takes," Holbrook said earnestly.

"You have to find him first."

"Together, we can do that. All I need is your assurance that the favors go both ways."

"The same as always, eh?"

"That's right."

"You scratch my back—"

"Both ways," Holbrook repeated.

"Let's do it then."

A phone chirped in the booth, and Quarrie took the call. His face went hard ten seconds in, and he cut off the call without saying a word.

"No time for breakfast now," he said. "That trouble's started in my own backyard."

New Kingston, City Centre

SOMETIMES GORILLAS NEEDED ACCOUNTANTS…lawyers, too. The Viper Posse was rolling in money, coming and going from black-market sources and highly placed sponsors. They required sage advice where investments were concerned and when its members found themselves in court. Enter the bean counters and legal eagles, scooping up whatever they could for themselves.

The firm of Boothe, Cassells and Moncrief occupied the fourteenth floor of a high-rise located at the corner of Tower and Princess Streets. Bolan peered into its windows from a rooftop opposite, through the scope on his AS50. Corner offices meant partners, hence prime targets in his game of hit and run.

He'd checked the firm beforehand, learning that they only handled posse clients, staying well away from small investors and the legal clientele whose cases ran toward traffic accidents, divorces and the like. Their lawyers had gone to court for thirteen murderers within the past six months, winning acquittals for eleven. The accountants channeled millions into secret bank accounts, legitimate investments, and the pockets of selected politicians who could help the posse grow and prosper.

Bad news all around, and now the tab was due.

The fat man sitting in the northeast corner office was Aaron Moncrief, recognizable from his smirking photo on the firm's website. Bolan zeroed in on his jowly face from ninety yards—the next best thing to point-blank with the AS50's telescopic sight—and stroked the rifle's trigger, sending 750 grains of armor-piercing death downrange. The office window rippled but did not implode. Behind his massive desk, Moncrieff's round head erupted into gray-and-crimson mist before he toppled over backward in his high-backed swivel chair.

While rolling thunder echoed over Princess Street, startling pedestrians below, Bolan shifted to the window at the building's southeast corner. Henry Boothe was on his feet, after a fashion, leaning on his desk while talking—maybe flirting—with a pretty secretary half his age. He hadn't heard the first shot, insulated in his air-conditioned private sanctum, or perhaps dismissed it as a backfire from the street.

He didn't hear the next one, either.

Bolan fired a second time, aiming precisely so there'd be no danger to the secretary, going for the target's torso to avoid a swarm of bone chips flying toward her face. His .50 BMG round drilled the office window neatly, still no shatter from the tempered glass, and entered Boothe's shoulder, passing on to clip his pulmonary artery and leave his heart a spurting chunk of ravaged meat inside.

Enough.

The second shot had people peering up toward Bolan's rooftop aerie, and he registered that it was time to go. He stowed the AS50 in its case, roughly the size of a golf bag, and double-timed back to the service stairs.

A job well-done, and he could almost feel the shock waves spreading now.

New Kingston, City Centre

DETECTIVE SERGEANT CLANCY RECKFORD wasn't used to tidy murders. In his twelve years with the Jamaica Constabulary Force he'd seen machete hackings, some dismemberment, bodies run over half a dozen times and more gang shootings than he cared to think about. The latter cases—like the one he'd just come from, out in Arnett Gardens—normally involved a frenzied burst of automatic fire or shotgun blasts, leaving a clutch of mangled bodies on the pavement or inside some cheap apartment. That was how the Shower Posse had earned its name, by showering its enemies with lead. Various competitors had emulated that approach to the extent that Kingston's streets were little better than a shooting gallery.

But this was different.

The homicides at Boothe, Cassells and Moncrief were almost surgically precise. Two long-range shots and two men dead, the one almost decapitated while his partner's blood and other vital fluids had evacuated from an exit wound the size of Reckford's fist.

High caliber, a marksman on the roof directly opposite.

If Reckford peered through Aaron Moncrief's punctured window, he could see a uniformed patrolman on that rooftop, standing guard over the cartridge casing he'd found. The Special Operations Unit was en route to analyze the scene, collect forensic evidence, but Reckford knew the basic facts already.

And he knew the victims by their reputation, lawyers and accountants who were well-paid servants of the Viper Posse, meaning that Jerome Quarrie had owned their souls. Reckford wished he could see where they were now: in heaven, hell, or simply floating in eternal darkness.

At least, he thought, they're off the street.

Just like the Viper Posse thugs who'd been shot to ribbons in The Jungle.

Were the crimes connected? Reckford didn't trust coincidence, although he knew that some things simply happened. Once, he'd seen a pedophile run over by a bus while in pursuit of an intended victim. He'd seen two members of a single family killed in separate and unrelated shootings on the same weekend. The murder rate in Kingston was so high that anything was possible.

But Reckford looked around him now and knew that something serious was happening.

Perhaps he'd have a word with Quarrie and take along a team from the Motorized Patrol in case of trouble. But confronting posse leaders meant he'd have to get permission from his superintendent. Posse business was so inextricably related to the country's politics these days—a national disgrace in Reckford's view—that special rules applied to "bothering" the top-tier gangsters. Short of evidence condemning a posse leader for murder, in front of witnesses, they were protected from invasions of their privacy.

Officially, at least.

But *watching* Quarrie was another matter altogether. No one could control who Reckford looked at, in the course of any given day. And if surveillance helped him solve the latest rash of murders, he might have the case wrapped up before the ever-present lawyers had a chance to make a mess of things.

Ministry of National Security, Oxford Road, Kingston

DALE HOLBROOK SHOWED ID to a pair of armed guards at the entrance to an underground garage, waiting while one of them checked his name against a list of expected visitors on an iPad. When that was done, he passed through into shade that smelled like oil and gasoline, parked his embassy compact in a visitor's space, locked it up and set the alarm. He rode the elevator skyward, ascending through the National Commercial Bank building's north tower, where Jamaica's Ministry of National Security operated from a third-floor suite of offices.

He'd called ahead, of course. Jamaican politicians didn't like to be surprised, particularly with bad news. The fact that Holbrook came to help should ease the way, but he'd learned that certain islanders obstructed logical discourse simply because they could.

And one such man was Perry Campbell, undersecretary of the MNS.

Holbrook passed through a security checkpoint in the building's lobby, then another on the third floor as he left the elevator, finally reaching the office where a stern-faced receptionist checked her own list of appointments, grudgingly admitting that he had the date and time correct. Holbrook sat in the waiting room and thumbed a dog-eared travel magazine until he finally was summoned to the undersecretary's lair.

Five minutes late, of course.

In half a dozen meetings, he'd never caught a glimpse of Campbell's smile. Today was no exception. Campbell was frowning slightly as he waved Holbrook in the direction of an empty chair before his desk. No handshake, either, which was out of character.

"You've caught me at a hectic time," Campbell said. "Many problems to be dealt with."

"And I'm hoping I can help with some of them. Are you recording this?"

Campbell feigned injured innocence. "Recording? I'm sure I don't know what—"

"I can't discuss this if you're taping it," Holbrook cut in.

Campbell regarded him with frank suspicion, then slipped one hand underneath his desk. "All right," he said. "What secrets do you have for me today."

Only half-sure the recorder was switched off, Holbrook decided to proceed. "I'm here about the Viper Posse."

"Oh?" Same old charade.

"As you're aware from other conversations—" getting it on record, just in case "—they have provided useful information to my people in the past. Just as they've helped your party at election time."

No audible response to that.

"They're coming under fire," Holbrook said, "source unknown as yet. They've lost a lot of people in Miami, and the trouble's started here. A shooting at The Jungle, as I understand it."

Campbell's meaty shoulders slumped a little. "And another in New Kingston," he replied. "A legal and accounting firm."

"Connected?"

"Almost certainly."

"I've spoken to the man," Holbrook said. No names mentioned, whether the recorder was switched off or not.

"We'll be collaborating to resolve the problem, and I'm hoping for assistance from your office."

"We're assigned to solve the crimes," Campbell replied, stating the obvious.

"Of course. But there is solved, and then, there's *solved*."

"A fine distinction that escapes me, I'm afraid."

"Does it?"

"Perhaps, if I knew what you have in mind…"

"A parallel investigation with a permanent solution. Minimal publicity, if any. Zero internal leaks to TV Jamaica or any print media."

"What would I tell my superiors?" Campbell inquired.

"Whatever suits you. All they really want is peace and quiet, am I right?"

"And what would I have to do for this peace and quiet?"

"Nothing, literally. Go through all the motions of a usual investigation, but make sure your men don't get in anybody's way."

"Mmm-hmm. For which, I would receive…?"

"Aside from acclamation? How about ten grand?"

"Twenty sounds more agreeable."

"So, split the difference? Fifteen?"

Campbell sat back. Still didn't smile. "A swift solution is imperative," he said.

"You're preaching to the choir," Holbrook assured him. "'Speedy' is my middle name."

Passmore Town, Kingston

FULL DARK MASKED BOLAN as he climbed a fire escape on Potters Row, west of Kingston's General Penitentiary. The metal stair creaked underneath his weight, but Bolan wasn't worried about anybody hearing him. His target, on the fourth floor of an aging tenement, blared music from its partly opened windows to the alleyway outside.

And inside, Bolan knew, the night shift would be hard at work.

The loft had been converted to a cocaine cutting plant, where kilos from Colombia were "stepped on"—cut with anything from baking soda to baby laxatives—and re-packaged for street sale or freebased into crack.

Tonight, however, Quarrie's primo cutting plant was going out of business.

Bolan hunkered down on the landing just outside one of the open windows, listening to Shaggy sing "It Wasn't Me." No music connoisseur, per se, liked the beat and let the lyrics go, peering inside the loft to sort his targets out.

The cutting table was staffed by women dressed in thongs and surgical masks, nothing else, to keep them from inhaling or pilfering product. More drones at a second table handled packaging for street sales, scooping powder into little glassine envelopes. Farther back, a cooking station made the crack, its techies wearing headgear that resembled army-surplus gas masks. Circulating through the plant were half a dozen guards, the only people fully dressed, their automatic weapons shoulder-slung, eyes constantly shifting above paper masks.

How many altogether? Call it twenty-five.

Bolan felt no animosity toward any of the drones, beyond the fact that they were making misery for thousands. He knew about Jamaica's rate of poverty, the lure of relatively easy money for a single mother or a kid going to school, and he didn't care. They'd picked a dirty business, also dangerous. Sad to say, some might end up being collateral damage.

Tonight, the ones who lived could say they'd earned their pay.

He primed one of the L109A1 frag grenades and pitched it sideways, watching as it bounced once on the cutting table, then resumed its wobbling flight toward the cooking station. Bolan ducked well before it detonated in midair, the razored fragments of its casing slicing into bodies, lab equipment and the big room's redbrick walls. Women and men were crying out, some of them down and writhing on the floor, a rain of crystal powder falling over them.

Before the guards could work out what was happening, Bolan cut loose with his L85A1, firing short bursts that took them down wherever they were standing, fumbling with their weapons, blinking teary eyes and coughing. None of them enjoyed the sudden high, as bullets ripped into their heads, chests, torsos, and their lives winked out like dying candle flames.

Enough. He left the wage slaves to their own devices, scrambled back downstairs into the narrow alleyway, and north from there to reach his waiting rental car. He hadn't bribed a crew to watch the vehicle this time, just stashed it in the shadow of a service station long since closed. In moments, he was out of there and rolling toward his next appointment with the Viper Posse.

Hunting, as another drizzling tropical rain began to fall.

9

Passmore Town, Kingston

Sergeant Reckford stayed outside the cocaine plant and watched the cleanup crew. The corpses had already been removed, while wounded workers were conveyed to Kingston Public Hospital. The handful without open wounds, once they'd found their clothes and dressed themselves, were on their way to processing at the Elletson Road police station. Reckford hoped to interview them there, once they were booked.

Assuming the rash of killings slowed enough to give him time.

He'd given up on counting corpses. Reckford knew that only two of them, so far, would matter to his superiors, because the dead lawyers were affluent and shared their wealth with the politicians who controlled Jamaica's destiny. Their families would clamor for results, and for revenge. He was already taking heat for failing to provide a list of suspects in the crimes.

"Looks like somebody's doin' us a favor, Sergeant," a constable said in passing.

Reckford grunted, understanding how the man felt, still unwilling to endorse mass murder as a means of crime fighting. If that was all it took, why not dismiss the force and send in troops to scour Passmore Town and other districts like it, shooting anyone they caught out on the streets?

Corporal Walcott approached him, frowning at the sight of Reckford's solemn face. "Did you hear what the girls were saying?" he inquired.

"What girls?"

"The workers here."

"I haven't seen them yet."

"They claim the shooter was a white man. Crazy, eh?"

"What kind of white man?"

Walcott shrugged. "Who knows?"

"We need to make the rounds, find out if anybody else remembers seeing him."

"You take it seriously?"

"Is there any reason I shouldn't?"

"Well, there's the notion of a white man here, in Dunkirk. And the girls were rattled, maybe high from all the cocaine dust floating around."

"I'll judge that when I've spoken to them. In the meantime, start making the rounds."

"This neighborhood," Walcott reminded him, "no one sees anything. We're Babylon."

"It doesn't hurt to ask. They might give up a white man quicker than a yardie."

"If you say so."

"I've already said it."

Sensing Reckford's mood, the corporal retreated, saying, "Yes, sir. Right away."

Alone once more, Reckford hitched up his trousers, thinking for the hundredth time that he should wear suspenders to keep his Browning Hi-Power pistol from dragging them down on the right. He'd only fired his pistol twice on duty, in a dozen years, and neither of the men he'd shot had died, though one had lost a testicle.

Bad luck.

He peered into the lab again, determined that the cleanup might go on for hours yet, and turned away. He needed to confront the cutting plant's survivors, in particular the women who described a white man as the author of this latest mayhem. It was an anomaly demanding resolution, and it might lead to something larger than a simple turf war.

Might lead to trouble, if he didn't handle the investigation tactfully.

Indeed, might even get him killed.

Tinson Pen Aerodrome, Kingston

THE FLIGHT FROM Ian Fleming International in Boscobel was running late. Such things were not unusual, particularly when the aircraft was a drug flight bound from Barranquilla, on the north shore of Colombia, to Kingston by a zigzag route designed to fool authorities. It could have flown directly into Kingston, but that might have been too obvious, inviting trouble, even though substantial bribes had certainly been paid to guarantee a safe delivery.

Bolan was staked out on a 6th Street rooftop, with a clear view of the runway, end to end. He didn't mind a little extra waiting, sheltered as he was from prying eyes, and he'd secured his exit route. The AS50 lay beside him, resting on its adjustable bipod. He'd topped off the magazine, but didn't plan on using more than one or two rounds.

His target was a Learjet 29, registered to a Colombian corporation that only existed on paper, owned in fact by a prominent cartel.

Nothing could stop the flow of drugs, but tonight he would make a small dent in the trade.

The Lear was nineteen minutes late when it swooped into view, circling the airfield, looping into its approach. It would be landing head-on to the Executioner, rolling directly into Bolan's crosshairs from his rooftop stand, the next best thing to firing at a stationary.

He confirmed the jet's ID number, beginning with the "HK" prefix standard for Colombian aircraft, and settled into his AS50, lining up the shot. There was a moment when the Lear appeared to hover, just above the tarmac, with its landing gear deployed, and Bolan took his shot then, 750 grains of copper-jacketed annihilation ripping through the nose wheel, shredding rubber. It was nothing you'd notice from the cockpit, necessarily.

At least, until the jet touched down.

That was the moment all hell broke loose, the forty-eight-foot aircraft standing on its nose, kissing the asphalt, skidding that way for a hundred feet or so, before it flipped completely over onto its back. His second round drilled through one of the Learjet's long-range fuel tanks, touching off a fireball that consumed the plane, even as it continued sliding, grinding down the runway, losing bits and pieces of itself along the way.

How many men inside there? Two-man crews were standard on a Learjet 29; he couldn't say if they'd brought any help along for loading and unloading cargo. Either way, the cartel's hirelings knew what they were signing up for when they banked their pay. There were no heroes in the drug trade, only cannon fodder.

Bolan bagged his rifle, left the rooftop and went back to find his war.

Windward Road, Kingston

JEROME QUARRIE HADN'T FELT this close to panic since he was a small child, fighting to survive on Kingston's brutal streets. He'd overcome those childhood fears and built an empire for himself, but now, within twelve hours, he'd seen it threatened on all fronts, in Florida and now his own backyard.

Police were still investigating what had happened to the Learjet from Colombia. As slowly as the Jamaica Civil Aviation Authority worked, it could be weeks before they had a verdict on the crash, and even then it might be speculative, leaving vital questions glaringly unanswered.

Never mind.

Quarrie already knew why it had crashed. He couldn't say *exactly*, couldn't point to the weapon used, whether it was a bomb, a rocket, even sabotage, but it was clearly another in the series of attacks from an unknown enemy. The punishing assaults that would not stop until he'd identified his foes and crushed them into bloody, screaming pulp.

Beyond that, there was more bad news.

He was responsible for anything that happened to the Learjet and its cargo once it reached Jamaican soil. Quarrie had no contract with his suppliers, in the legal sense, but both sides understood the terms and they were carved in stone. His headstone, if he didn't pay what he owed for the consignment, even though the cargo was reduced to stinking ash.

He had a little breathing room, since no one was left to claim the money—after they were cooked on Tinson Pen's runway—but someone would come to collect before the week was out.

"Fire for you!" he bellowed, bringing two guards running. They stood gaping at him, until he turned on them and snarled, "What are you looking at? Get out of here!"

They turned and fled, exchanging troubled glances. Quarrie went back to pondering the problems that confronted him. First, he had to find the cash to pay off his suppliers. Second, and by far the more important, he needed to learn who was attacking him and put a stop to it.

Failure on either front would doubtless mean his death.

"Trevor, get in here!" he shouted, fuming as he waited fifteen seconds for his chief lieutenant to appear.

"What, Boss?" Trevor asked him, eyes sweeping the room as if in search of hidden enemies.

"We need to get our hands on cash, before the damned Colombians come calling."

"How much?"

Quarrie told him, watched his eyes go wide then narrow down to slits before he spoke again. "And find whoever's doing this to us! You hear me? Find him now!"

Ministry of National Security, Oxford Road

PERRY CAMPBELL HATED WORRYING. He hadn't worked so long and so hard, running the maze of dirty politics, leaving his friends and enemies behind him, only to have some cheap yardie and a damned American undo him now. The trouble was that he couldn't see a way to rid himself of either one, without doing some major damage to himself.

Holbrook was CIA. He made no secret of it in their private conversations, even though he posed as some kind of attaché at the US embassy. Holbrook must know the facts of Campbell's dealings with the Viper Posse, on behalf of the People's National Party. That collaboration would raise few eyebrows in Kingston, but if broadcast internationally—say, on CNN, or worse yet, on Fox News—it could result in his removal. He'd be replaced with someone equally corrupt, if not more so, but Campbell could not live on irony.

He needed cash and plenty of it, to maintain the lifestyle he cherished.

And if Quarrie thought Campbell was failing him, hundreds of obliging candidates stood waiting in the wings for any government position they could grab. Campbell might get a warning, might lose a family member to an apparent accident or "random" shooting, and if that failed to correct his lapse, he would be killed.

Sipping a glass of Wray & Nephew rum, letting it set his guts on fire, he saw two ways out of the snare that held him. One, the obvious, was to perform as Quarrie and the CIA expected, fielding constables, inspectors, whatever it took to solve the mystery of who was killing Quarrie's men and why. It hardly mattered who got credit for the execution of their tormentors, as long as it was done and nothing leaked to the media that could embarrass either of his sponsors.

That was the ideal solution to his misery.

The other was to cut and run.

First thing tomorrow morning, he could drop into his bank, empty his account, clean out his safe-deposit box, and catch the next flight out of Kingston going—where?

That was the point where Campbell's backup plan broke down. He thought it might be possible to outrun Quarrie and his posse, somewhere halfway round the world, perhaps. But hiding from the CIA? That was a fantasy. They eavesdropped on the phones of billions, scoured emails by the terabyte per second, gleaning every secret on the planet. They could trace him anywhere and punish him for running out with debts unpaid, his duties unfulfilled.

Campbell had issued orders to the JCF's commissioner, resplendent in his uniform, a Cuban cigar protruding from his fleshy face. All other pending cases must immediately take a backseat to the search for this madman on the prowl.

The bottom line: find him, or them, without further delay, or be prepared to sacrifice yourself, give up your cushy job and all its perks, to someone smarter, more efficient. And if that were not sufficient motivation, there was the matter of an offshore bank account bursting with cash that couldn't be explained.

The message was received. It stuck. But would it be enough?

Campbell considered praying, but he'd forgotten how.

And who would listen, anyway?

Greenwich Town, Kingston

"YOU FOUND THESE HERE?"

The corporal nodded. "Where you see the markers, Sergeant."

Two small plastic pyramids, bright red, like Lilliputian traffic cones, lay on the flat rooftop where Clancy Reckford stood, staring off toward the runway of Tinson Pen Aerodrome. In each hand, he held a plastic sandwich bag, labeled in Magic Marker with the date, address and case number. Inside each bag was an identical .50-caliber Browning Machine Gun cartridge. If he opened the bags, Reckford knew he would smell the gunpowder, a heady aroma of death.

"Good shooting," he observed. "What do you make the distance, Corporal? Eight hundred yards?"

"At least, sir."

The Learjet's wreckage had been doused with foam, then photographed before a crane hoisted it clear of the runway. Life went on, except for those inside the twisted, blackened aircraft, and Tinson Pen could not have other planes plummeting out of the sky as their fuel tanks ran dry from circling and waiting.

Back to business as usual, more or less. Pay no attention to that black smudge on the runway.

It must have been quite a show, though. Two shots had turned the Lear into a tumbling crematorium. They wouldn't know how many people were inside for some time yet, until inspectors from the Civil Aviation Authority had studied it from every angle, hemming and hawing, snapping their photographs, scribbling on clipboards. Only then could firefighters employ their various hydraulic extrication tools to crack the fuselage and make their way inside.

Reckford, meanwhile, already knew some things about the plane. The aerodrome's control tower had given the make and model—an impressive Learjet 29—and had supplied the registration number that was burned off in the blaze. That led him to the corporation that held title to the aircraft, in Colombia, and there the trail stopped dead.

Which told him something else.

The plane had been transporting contraband, most likely drugs, but someone with a keen eye and a mighty weapon was determined that it should not land. The same person, he knew with perfect certainty, had executed two senior partners at Boothe, Cassells and Moncrief. There might be several .50-caliber sniper rifles floating around Kingston this night, but Reckford would have bet his pension that only one rested in such expert hands.

And did those hands belong to a white man, by any chance? Was it a hopeless stretch to link these snipings with the earlier attacks on operations of the Viper Posse?

Reckford didn't think so.

And if he was right, what did it mean? The easy answer was some kind of turf war, starting in South Florida and jumping to the islands when the rivals Quarrie had offended didn't think he'd learned his lesson. White gangsters, then, or some cartel that would employ white killers, probably ex-military men.

Russians or Chechens? Albanians or Serbs? Sicilians? Quarrie bought cocaine from a Colombian cartel, but was a rival outfit squeezing out his suppliers?

All fair possibilities. And yet, none of them struck his mind as satisfactory.

Dig deeper, then, he thought. Track down the weapon first.

Another Herculean task, but he already had a few ideas.

Half Way Tree Road, Kingston

THE POSH JAMAICA FLAME NIGHTCLUB was not a typical Viper Posse operation, but ownership traced back to Jerome Quarrie, all the same. The club was a cash cow, ignored by police while the payoffs kept coming, and none of the gamblers complained of a rigged game or rip-off. Most players took losses in stride—even expected them, in the case of degenerate gamblers—and anyone who complained too loudly could generally be dissuaded by Quarrie's goon squad, out of sight from the good-time crowd.

Bolan left his Camry at a restaurant on Chelsea Avenue and walked a short block to the club. He'd left most of his arsenal locked in the car, wearing the Glock 18 in its shoulder rig with a lone grenade clipped to his belt in back, as a last-ditch precaution. If all went well, he wouldn't have to fire a shot this time.

If not…

The Jamaica Flame's casino was a backroom operation, two stout guards on the door, but Bolan hadn't come to place a bet or rob the players. A hostess met him in the foyer, offered him a table, then directed him toward the manager's office instead when he showed her a fake business card from a liquor supply house. It meant nothing to her. She'd expect to see him leaving within minutes, having learned that the Jamaica Flame was well fixed for booze.

He found the office, door marked "PRIVATE," with another guard on station. No one else was close enough to see them as he pulled the Glock with its extended magazine and silencer, disarmed the guard and ordered him inside.

Well trained, the sentry still took time to knock and wait until a gruff voice asked, "Who's that?"

"You have a visitor," the guard said, and led Bolan inside, to find a lean man rising from behind a cluttered desk.

"What's this?" the manager demanded. "Are you crazy?"

"I've heard it said," Bolan replied, waggling his pistol toward a safe that occupied one corner of the office. "Open that and clean it out. You're going broke tonight."

"You *are* crazy. The men who own this place aren't ones to mess with."

"Just get on with it."

The manager opened the safe, revealing stacks of bundled currency. "What now?" he asked. "You gonna stuff your pockets?"

"No. You'll have a satchel for deliveries. Let's see it. That, and nothing else."

Scowling, the man retreated to his desk, reached underneath it, and retrieved a Halliburton briefcase large enough to hold most of the money in the safe.

"All right," Bolan said. "Load it up. Start with the big bills. First trick you try will be your last."

When it was filled and latched, he took the case and nodded for the angry-looking guard to join his boss behind the desk. They stood two feet apart until he told them, "Closer. Don't be shy."

The lookout shuffled closer to his manager, not liking it, and stopped just as their shoulders touched.

"Where's the alarm?" Bolan inquired.

"There isn't one," the lean man lied.

"Okay."

Almost regretfully, he knocked both men out—a swift crack to the forehead with the butt of the Glock—and bound their wrists with plastic ties. Bolan locked the office door behind him and passed the hostess on his way back to the street. He hadn't counted what was in the briefcase, but knew it could be the equivalent of millions in American dollars.

Enough to get Quarrie's attention, at least.

Enough to ramp his paranoia up another notch, and maybe put him on the run.

10

Tivoli Gardens, Kingston

Jerome Quarrie was going back to his roots. It was depressing, but he couldn't think of any better place to hide, and the thought of fleeing the capital entirely, leaving all that he'd won and built, was more than he could bear. Tivoli Gardens had concealed men of his stature in the past, and could again.

He traveled in the middle of a three-car caravan, his Lincoln MKS limousine sandwiched between two carbon-copy Lexus LX 570 sport utility vehicles, each seating five well-armed soldiers. With four in the limo, that made fourteen guards for his mobile escort, plus a dozen waiting at his fortified bunker, a house on Deece Avenue, two blocks from May-Pen Cemetery.

Quarrie had contributed more than his share of customers to May-Pen over time, but he had no fear of their ghosts rising to trouble him while he was in the neighborhood. He'd already made the necessary sacrifice—although, in truth, it hadn't helped him yet; another disappointment grating on his nerves—and on a chain around his neck he wore a talisman prepared by *papaloi* Usain Dalhouse. The amulet was simple, unobtrusive, hollow glass surrounded by a modest silver trim. Inside it lay a stub of dark material that might have been old leather, but wasn't.

The withered foreskin of a firstborn son, offered to the *orishas* within moments of his birth.

Quarrie believed in the Obeah charm because it hadn't failed him yet. Since he'd purchased it, a special order, Quarrie had survived seven attempts upon his life. On only one occasion was he injured, and the wound had been a graze, the only one of nineteen bullets fired to even touch his flesh. The amulet had been expensive, certainly, but what price could he place on life itself?

The question made him smile, despite his sour mood. Quarrie regarded his own life as priceless. But the lives of others? Not so much.

"Two minutes, Boss," his driver said. The men around him shifted in their seats, holding their weapons ready. Quarrie watched the blocks of run-down flats and houses pass.

"I hate this place," he said, to no one in particular. Since it wasn't a question, no one answered him.

Thugs of all ages prowled the district's streets, living off women, off the dole, from all varieties of crime. In every way that mattered, Tivoli had made him what he was today—a drug lord and a hunted man.

But who was hunting him, and why?

The holdup at Jamaica Flame was part of it, no doubt. The hostess had described a white assailant and handed over his supposed business card. He was a chimera, slipping in and out of focus, baffling Quarrie with his expertise and seeming lack of motive.

This was war, but what had brought it on?

He would have liked to put the blame on Winston Channer, dead and gone now, but that didn't solve his problem. Only when he met his adversary face-to-face, and heard his screams for mercy, would he understand the plague that threatened him.

And then?

He would eradicate the men behind the soldier, make them rue the day they ever thought to challenge Quarrie on his own turf.

"We're here, Boss," his driver said as the caravan rolled to a halt. His guards bailed out, made no attempt to hide their weapons as they formed a corridor of flesh and steel between the curb and Quarrie's sanctuary.

Raising one hand to the amulet, he whispered, "Fire for you!" and rushed into the house.

Windward Road, Kingston

BOLAN DROVE BY QUARRIE'S place, having a look, but couldn't see beyond the walls surrounding it. He'd phoned ahead to have a chat with Quarrie, rattle him a little, but the landline rang and rang with no pickup. He could let it go for now, or stop and find out whether Quarrie was at home.

Why not?

One block past the house, he turned south onto Sea Breeze Avenue and found a place to park the Camry, cutting through the backyard of a house sporting a for-sale sign out front, dark windows watching as he passed. After jumping the chain-link fence in back, he was standing on the grass border of a waterway that ran from Kingston Harbor toward downtown. He followed it until it slipped under a bridge at Windward Road, then he turned east toward his target.

Bolan scouted Quarrie's privacy wall on foot, found no barbed wire or other obstacles on top of it, and nothing that resembled cameras or motion sensors. Chancing it, he scrambled to the top and froze there, checking out the property inside, trying a dog whistle he carried with him. When the ultrasonic note brought no response, he used a pencil flashlight on the ground below, observed no traps and dropped down to earth.

The house hulked up in front of him, no lights burning inside that he could see. Bolan started on a circuit of the silent building, Glock in hand, he had completed half the trip before he reached the back porch and a yellow bug light suddenly went on. He crouched in shadow, waiting motionless until the back door opened and two Rasta types stepped out, both wearing automatic weapons shoulder-slung.

Rolling the dice, he dropped the last one through the door, a silent head shot, leaping forward even as the dead man fell, clubbing his comrade to the ground. Bolan disarmed him, kneeling on his neck, the still-warm silencer pressed tight against his cheek.

"How many more of you inside?" Bolan demanded.

"Nobody."

"Where's Quarrie?"

"Gone."

"Gone where?"

"I don't know nothin'!"

Bolan ground the silencer into his ear. "Once more."

"I'm not a rat!"

"You want to live, the question's simple."

"Hell with you, you—"

Bolan shifted, shot him through the fleshy part of his thigh, and listened to the squeal that should have brought help coming from the house.

None came.

"Once more," he said.

"Okay! Don't shoot no more!"

Again Bolan asked, "Where's Quarrie?"

"Gone to his place, out in Tivoli."

"Tivoli Gardens?"

"That's right."

"What's the address?"

"I don't know that. Can find it, but I couldn't say the number."

"Street name?"

A painful, frantic head-shake. "No! I ain't lyin!"

"Okay," Bolan replied, and rose.

The dread was fast, even with a bullet in his upper thigh, whipping around, drawing a knife from somewhere, lunging. Bolan shot him through the forehead, left him there, and jogged back toward the wall.

If Quarrie was beyond his reach for now, he'd try the Viper Posse's number two.

Greenwich Town, Kingston

KINGSTON LOANS WAS Clancy Reckford's second stop. He'd tried another dealer first, got nowhere even when he turned the heat up, and had three more on his list before he called it quits. It was too early to dismiss his idea as a waste of time just yet.

The place was open late, no real surprise, since people often had a sudden need for money in the middle of the night. There was drinking to do, drugs to score, sex to be bargained for. Some of the pawn shop's customers were honest men and women, short of cash, who came to trade their rings, bracelets and such for currency. Others were thieves, unloading stolen merchandise.

And some came seeking guns.

Reckford entered the shop and saw that Simon Reid himself was at the register. They didn't know each other, but the pawnbroker had been arrested once—receiving stolen property, the case later dismissed—and he'd changed little since his mug shot had been taken, seven years before. He also had sharp eyes, knowing a copper when he saw one, even when the officer was out of uniform.

"Detective! Welcome to my humble place of business."

"Sergeant," Reckford said.

"Congratulations. Have you come to purchase something? An engagement ring, perhaps, or—"

Reckford dropped the sandwich bag in front of Reid. The .50-caliber cartridge inside it made a loud *clack* on the glass display case filled with rings and watches. Reid peered at it, shook his head and said, "No, sir. I don't have anything like that."

"It's one of four I've found today," Reckford remarked, as if Reid hadn't spoken. "Two killed a couple of the city's most important businessmen, the sort with well-placed friends. The others made a bloody mess at Tinson Pen. You may have seen it on the television?"

"No, sir."

"Strange and terrible. A private plane destroyed, with three men dead inside it. They're unidentified so far, but we believe they were Colombians. Employees of a major drug cartel."

"And what has that to do with me?"

"The businessmen, you understand, are deemed important. They have partners, friends in government, who have demanded that we leave no stone unturned to find the killer. As for the Colombians, they won't consult us, but they have their own ways of investigating and resolving things."

Reid's eyes were shifting nervously. "Why are you telling me all this?"

"Consider it a warning."

"Warning?"

He took a chance. "Once they get hold of you, you'll be beyond our help."

"And why would anybody come for me?"

"Because you have a certain reputation, Simon. Rumor has it that you deal in guns. A little sideline, just to make ends meet in these hard times."

"I mighta done, sometime."

"And recently?"

"I'm not a wanted man. Got no charges against me."

"Yet. But if I call in for a warrant to go through this place, I'm betting we'll find stolen merchandise. And guns."

"You gonna lock me up?"

"That all depends on what you tell me next."

"All right. I sold something like this, a while ago."

"How long?"

"Was yesterday."

"Who bought this?"

"I didn't ask his name. Paid cash, you know?"

"Then describe him."

"White. Taller than you. Sounded American, not British."

"And you'd know him if you met again?"

"Why would I see him again?"

"If he came back here for more…supplies."

He nodded. "I guess so."

Reckford handed Reid a business card. "If he returns, call me at once. You understand?"

"Yeah, sure. What about the other thing?"

"I'll think about it," Reckford told him. "If you let me down, all this can go away. You, too."

"I hear you."

Leaving the pawn shop with his best lead yet, although a slim one, Reckford thought he had a chance to break the case. And if he failed?

Then, he supposed, the Viper Posse should prepare for all-out war.

Norman Gardens, Kingston

TREVOR SEAGA HAD not been invited to join Jerome Quarrie's retreat. It irked him, but he understood in principle. A symbol of authority must remain visible to keep the troops in line, and even more so, to prevent the posse's countless enemies from thinking they had an opening to strike against their betters. As the outfit's second in command, he was the natural choice to remain, conveying orders from the posse's absent leader.

It might even work to his advantage.

Quarrie's disappearing act at such a time, when everything he owned was under fire, made him look weak. Seaga had the power to refute or to encourage that impression, to strengthen Quarrie's image or to undermine it. At the moment, he was thinking of himself and wondering—not for the first time—whether he might be the better man to lead an empire, after all.

But first, he had to salvage what was left.

There had already been a phone call from Colombia, not threatening per se, but asking in a grim, no-nonsense way when final compensation for the latest shipment would be made. Seaga knew the rules and had not argued. He promised that the cash would be forthcoming, and reminded his suppliers of exactly how the shipment had been lost.

Not that they gave a damn.

That was one problem. The more pressing one, of course, was tracking down the man or men responsible for all the posse's troubles of the past few days. The *white* man or men, which made it even worse. It was an insult to the Viper Posse, and to Rastafarians worldwide.

It was intolerable, and it had to be stopped.

Seaga had a few ideas on how to do that. Police were already examining records of recent arrivals at Jamaica's three international airports, and officers on the posse's payroll would report any promising hits. Meanwhile—

Seaga heard his doorbell chime and stiffened in his swivel chair, stretching a hand out toward the drawer that held a .45-caliber MAC-10 machine pistol. His hand was resting on the weapon when his doorman knocked and stepped into the office, wide mouth drooping in a frown.

"Babylon is here," he said.

"How many? Do they have a warrant?"

"No, Boss. Just one guy."

Trevor relaxed and closed the drawer. "So show him in," he replied.

THERE WAS AN ELEMENT of danger, Reckford realized, in visiting Seaga at his home on Harbour Road. Particularly when he'd brought no backup, and had told no one at headquarters where he was going. At the time, it had seemed logical. He wasn't planning to provoke a confrontation, and had no idea who he could trust among his supervisors. Any one of them might tip Seaga off that he was coming, and the trip would be a waste of time.

Now he was in and following a tall, slope-shouldered posse member, obviously armed, along a corridor where others glared and blew smoke at him as he passed. Before he reached his destination at the far end of the hallway, Reckford had acquired a pleasant buzz.

Seaga's office was spacious, with broad windows facing a garden and the thickly wooded mountains rising east of Kingston. Seated at a desk, the windows at his back, Seaga made no move to rise as Reckford entered and the soldier shut the door behind him.

"What brings you here?" he asked.

"I'm Sergeant Reckford, JCF." He was reaching for his credentials as he spoke.

"I don't need to see that. You already showed it to my man."

"May I sit down?"

Seaga frowned and nodded toward a pair of chairs facing his desk. Reckford chose one of them and sat. "I'm looking for your boss," he said.

"My boss? Who's that?"

Reckford allowed himself a smile. "Jerome Quarrie, unless something's become of him that I don't know about."

"He's fine, last I heard."

"But not available to speak with the police?"

Seaga shrugged and spread his hands. "What can I tell you? He don't check with me before he goes on holiday."

"A holiday, with all that's going on? How stupid do you think I am?"

"Don't know. Just met you." He was grinning.

Reckford had to smile at that. "This killing must be bad for business," he said. "And that plane from Colombia was quite a loss."

"To somebody else," Seaga said. "Not my plane."

"I suspect the owners will be after payback, one way or another."

"Maybe so. Nothing to me."

"Not even if they thought you were responsible?"

Seaga frowned. "Why would they think that?"

"Who knows? Some kind of power play against your boss, let's say. He might not like that, either."

"He knows better."

"But if that was the *official* theory, if someone from Narcotics mentioned it in passing, say, to Quarrie or to Interpol, who knows where it might go from there?"

"What do you want?" Seaga demanded.

"I told you. A word with your boss. Failing that, cooperation to resolve the problem Kingston, and your posse, is facing."

"Not my problem. Word on the street says you should be out lookin' for a white man."

"And you wouldn't know who that might be? Who sent him?"

"You want me guessing now?"

"I'm open to whatever information or suspicion you might have," Reckford replied.

Seaga chewed on that a moment—literally, gnawing on his lower lip—and then leaned forward, elbows on his desktop, lowering his voice. "So, if I told you—"

When his head exploded, it was a complete, stunning surprise. Reckford was conscious of a *clink*, glass breaking, then Seaga's skull erupted like a melon with a cherry bomb inside it, spraying blood across the desk and into Reckford's face.

IT WAS A RELATIVELY easy shot: two hundred yards, flat roof beneath him, AS50 steady on its bipod, no crosswise wind requiring any compensation. He'd arrived on Harbour Road, staked out his stand, and quickly found Trevor Seaga's office with its windows facing eastward and the Viper Posse's number two relaxing at his desk, back to the fate awaiting him.

Maybe "relaxing" wasn't right. Seaga would have plenty on his mind, enough to give a normal person ulcers, though a psychopath was sometimes better under stress. No human feeling to distract him from the task at hand, unless fear had begun to put down roots.

Fear, or a mobster's normal greed.

Reaching Seaga for a chat had been impractical. Bolan was opting for a simple rub-out, one more blow to stagger Quarrie, but he hesitated, finger on the AS50's trigger, when a visitor arrived. The new guy looked like a cop, a first impression reinforced when he reached for a wallet or a badge case, right hand slipping underneath his blazer till Seaga waved him off. He sat, then, and the two of them began to talk.

Bolan wished he could have bugged the room. He wished he was a lip-reader, which would've let him pick up half the conversation going on down there.

Wishes and horses, Bolan thought, and held his fire, watching the officer spar with Seaga, neither of them giving any ground as far as he could see. But then, Seaga had leaned forward on his elbows, ducked his head like someone who was about to whisper something confidential to his uninvited guest.

And Bolan couldn't have that. If Seaga was about to give up his boss, sell him to the law, it could put Quarrie out of reach. From there, the case would drag through court for years, with ample opportunities for Quarrie to escape from custody, retaliate against his traitorous lieutenant, and perhaps touch off another bloody war in Kingston.

No.

He took a deep breath, released half of it and held the rest. His index finger squeezed the AS50's trigger, rode the recoil, eye frozen on the reticle of its scope. Downrange, a half-inch hole appeared in the glass of Seaga's mirror, a micro-second before the posse leader's head exploded, dreadlocks flailing like the tentacles of some demented squid in its death throes. He dropped facedown onto the desktop, while his visitor recoiled, painted in blood.

Bolan broke down the rifle, bagged it and was in his Camry on the street below before he heard a siren wailing, drawing closer. Others followed, and he watched from a safe distance while the officers went through the motions, tussling with Seaga's bodyguards at first, then cuffing them in order to conduct their crime-scene search.

And he was watching as the first cop on the scene departed, leaving higher-ranking members of the JCF in charge. The plainclothes cop drove off alone.

With Bolan on his tail.

11

Windward Road, Kingston

At first, Bolan thought the cop was heading back to head-quarters on Lower Elletson Road, but instead, he pulled in to the parking lot of an all-night diner near Bellevue Hospital. Bolan let him clear the lot and take a seat inside, a window booth, sitting alone, then waited in the Camry, watching to find out if anybody else was coming. It gave him time to wonder what the officer's story was, while weighing the pros and cons of a meeting.

The upside: if it went well, he could get the information he needed to find Quarrie, and might gain an ally in the bargain. Bolan didn't plan on wooing any honest law-men over to the vigilante side, but if a contact bought him time, a little combat stretch, it couldn't hurt.

The downside: if the cop was straight, he might be *too* straight to allow for any compromise. Confronted with the man who'd been spilling Viper Posse blood all over Kingston, he might feel obliged to end it, drawing down on Bolan, either killing him or hauling him away to jail. In either case, Bolan could only use nonlethal means to get away. Killing a cop was out of bounds, no matter what else he'd done.

The *other* downside: if the cop was dirty, on the Viper Posse's payroll, he still might attempt a move on Bolan, either for his gangland paymasters or on his own account, to solve the rash of crimes and make himself look good.

Again, the same restriction applied, since Bolan drew no line between good cops and bad, in terms of using deadly force.

Watching the lone man place his order with a slim Latino waitress, Bolan wished he'd bought a Taser when he'd stopped at Kingston Loans. He made a mental note to have one handy in the future, though the idea did no good at all right now.

How would he pitch it? Introduce himself by some assumed name, or remain anonymous? Once he'd been seen, the cop could always get together with a sketch artist, or maybe check the CCTV feed at Norman Manley International. Names were irrelevant at that point, and his hours on the island would be numbered.

They could talk, and he would see what happened next. Worse come to worst, a simple threat might buy him time enough to slip away before the cop raised an alarm. Say he was in a sniper's crosshairs while they spoke, for instance, and wouldn't be clear for—what? Ten minutes afterward?

Better.

Bolan hoped threats wouldn't be necessary, though. He didn't mind squeezing a dirty cop, or sending one to prison, but he hoped the solitary diner would surprise him, would turn out to be a decent man with some of his ideals intact, if bruised and battered by experience.

You might say Bolan was prepared to stake his life on it.

Fed up with waiting in the dark, he left his car behind and went inside.

Tivoli Gardens, Kingston

WHEN THE NEWS CAME, it was bad. As usual, in recent days, but worse than most. Jerome Quarrie was not inclined to

measure it against the other shocks he'd received since the
Miami killings started, but it struck him close to home.

Trevor Seaga. Dead.

Not merely dead, but with his head blown off while sitting in his home, in Norman Gardens. If the enemy could
reach him there, was anyplace in Kingston truly safe?

Quarrie decided on the spot, before he even finished
talking to the officer of Babylon who'd called him with
the tip, that he must leave the capital. While Tivoli was
safer than the neighborhood Trevor had chosen to reside
in, it could just as easily become a death trap if he stayed
too long. To fight another day, he had to survive this one,
and that meant getting out.

Already shouting as he cut the cell link, Quarrie began
issuing orders, choosing who would come with him and
who would stay behind, making the place seem occupied
and worth a closer look from enemies. He needed time
now, a distraction, and his men could serve as decoys,
even if they'd been no good at tracking down his foe.

After he'd given his instructions, Quarrie made his private preparations. He already had the better part of half a
million American dollars packed in two small suitcases.
He'd armed himself and issued orders for his soldiers to
continue searching every corner of the capital until they
found the man responsible for murdering their comrades.
Spilled blood cried aloud for vengeance and he would not
rest until that cry was answered.

Or until his own blood was spilled.

But Quarrie thought he could lead best from a distance,
now. Violence had claimed his oldest living friend and
confidant. He needed time to think without the Reaper
knocking on his door, and room to breathe without the
smell of death assaulting him. Kingston was soiled, and
he might have to take it back by force, but to do that, he
had to be alive.

When he'd finished seeing to his own needs for the road, Quarrie moved on to supervise the other preparations. He could call ahead, alert the force he kept in readiness at his intended hideaway, but why take chances? Cell phone calls could be plucked from thin air by any group or individual who had the right equipment. It was worse than talking on a landline, where at least protective measures could be taken to detect a tap.

No warning, then. He would surprise the soldiers at his outpost, trusting that they hadn't turned against him. Once established there, outside the city, he could focus on the problem of identifying and destroying his elusive enemy.

The white man.

Quarrie hoped he could catch the bastard alive, interrogate him and extract an explanation for the hell he'd wrought in Kingston and Miami. Quarrie needed names before he launched a war of retribution against those who'd attempted to destroy him and his empire.

And once they were identified, there would be nowhere on the planet they could hide.

Windward Road, Kingston

CLANCY RECKFORD WAS looking forward to his early breakfast, sautéed ackee and salt fish with a side order of johnnycakes. He smelled it cooking in the kitchen, had the diner to himself at this hour, except for the young waitress and the chef, until the door creaked at his back, a shadow fell across his coffee mug and someone sat down in the booth across from him.

A white man.

"Looked like you were on your own," the stranger said. "I thought it couldn't hurt for us to talk."

"Who are you?"

"Maybe later. For the moment, let's just say that I'm the man you're looking for."

"Oh, yes?"

"Boothe, Cassells and Moncrief," the man said. "Trevor Seaga."

"Am I supposed to recognize these names?"

"You've got Seaga on your jacket, just over the pocket where you keep your badge."

"But nothing on my gun, I think."

The man showed a weary smile. "That's one way you could go, but I don't like your chances." He had both hands underneath the table, out of sight. Reckford took care to leave his own hands on the tabletop, in plain view.

"So, this talk you mentioned. What is it about?"

The waitress interrupted them at that point, bringing Reckford's food. She asked the white man if he wanted anything and went to fetch a cup of coffee for him. Both of them sat silent until she returned, then left again.

"I thought we'd talk about the Viper Posse," the stranger said.

"Oh? In what respect?"

"They're going out of business. If you're not one of the cops protecting them, you might want to consider keeping a low profile for the next few hours. If you *are* protecting them, well…"

"I am not," Reckford replied, surprised to feel the heat rise in his face.

"I didn't think so. Maybe you could call in sick, or find another case to occupy you through tomorrow or the next day."

"You presume to give me orders?"

"Nope. Friendly advice."

"Who *are* you?" Reckford asked again.

"The 'who' is less important than the 'why.' Quarrie has overstepped his bounds. If you can tolerate his crimes in Kingston, that's your business, but he's been exporting drugs and murder. This is where it ends."

"Are you an agent of the US government?"

"A soldier, doing what he can with what he's got."

"A vigilante, then."

"Semantics don't concern me. When the smoke clears, I suspect there'll be inquiries into how and why the Viper Posse operated for so long without official intervention. Granted, most Jamaicans know the answer to that question from their personal experience and observations, but a crisis always agitates the politicians. Gives reformers cause and opportunity to speak up for a change."

"Your point is?"

"I'm no starry-eyed idealist," the man said. "All governments are riddled with corruption. But a shake-up's coming. Will it purify your country? Absolutely not. But certain people will be taking hits and losing jobs. A smart man knows enough to stay out of the crossfire."

"You'll forgive me," Reckford said, "if I don't believe you're here to offer me career advice."

The stranger laughed at that and sipped his coffee. "That's a good one. No, I'm hoping you might provide me with a piece of information, then get under cover for your own sake."

"Information?"

"An address in Tivoli Gardens where Quarrie would hide when he's worried."

"So you can kill him?"

And to that, no answer.

"What you're asking violates my oath of office and at least three laws that I can think of," Reckford said.

"I won't tell if you don't. As it is, you're swimming upstream in a sewer, getting nowhere."

More heat in Reckford's cheeks. He glowered at his

food, then pushed the plate away. "Bustamante Highway," he replied at last, and spoke a number.

"Thanks," the man said. "You have a card?"

Reckford surprised himself by pulling one from his pocket, passing it over the table. The stranger gave him one in turn, blank on both sides, except where he'd penned a phone number. That done, he rose and left some money on the table.

"Breakfast's on me," he said. "You ought to eat it while it's hot."

Embassy of the United States, Kingston

DALE HOLBROOK'S CELL PHONE buzzed and quivered in the right-hand pocket of his blazer, instantly distracting him from the cocktail in front of him. He'd ordered a Jamaican breeze—rum, pineapple juice, Angostura bitters, simple syrup and fresh ginger—but he hadn't had a chance to taste it yet, and now his intuition told him it might go to waste.

"Hello?"

"It's me." The voice he couldn't fail to recognize.

"We can't talk on this phone," he said, reminding Quarrie of a fact they'd discussed not once, but half a dozen times.

"It's an emergency!" the posse leader hissed at him. "I'm leaving Kingston tonight."

"That's good," Holbrook said, reaching for his drink. "Let things cool down a little and—"

"You have to help me!"

"I've been working on it," Holbrook said, dropping his voice another notch. "We *really* can't go into it right now."

"I don't care what you're working on," Quarrie replied. "I need to *see* you. We have to talk in person. It's the only way to know if I can trust you."

"Listen—"

"Will you come, or not?"

Jesus. "Where can I find you?" Holbrook asked.

"My place outside the city. You remember?"

Holbrook pictured the estate, said, "I remember."

"Don't take too long. We're running outta time."

The line went dead without so much as a goodbye. He cut the call from his end, downed his drink in one long swallow, barely tasting it until the rum and Angostura hit his stomach like a blast of napalm. Grimacing, he set the empty glass down, shaking his head at the embassy's bartender.

No refills.

He had a drive to make, and Holbrook wasn't looking forward to it. First, however, there were preparations to be made. He had to fetch the pistol from his desk, a Ruger LC9 autoloader never registered in the embassy's arms inventory, and make sure it was loaded.

What else would he need? A toothbrush? Screw it. He wouldn't pack extra clothes, because he didn't plan to be with Quarrie that long, or attract attention from the busybodies at the embassy by leaving with an overnight bag.

Should he write a note explaining where he'd gone, in case something went wrong? What would it say? Should he inscribe the envelope, "Open if I have disappeared"? What good would that do? The ambassador had zero jurisdiction outside of the embassy compound. He could suggest, entreat, cajole, but could not order or demand.

Useless.

Once he left the grounds and passed into the night, Holbrook would be on his own. It was exciting, in a way, but also frightening. With rum to take the edge off, he departed from the small salon and went to fetch his gun.

Windward Road, Kingston

BOLAN DROVE WESTWARD, heading toward Spanish Town Road. It was a relatively short drive, but he didn't rush it, taking time to think.

He had a feel for Clancy Reckford from their conversation. The sergeant seemed to be a good cop, within limits forced upon him by the agency he served, the city it protected, and his own background. Reckford had grown up knowing things worked a certain way in Kingston, probably believing they couldn't be changed short of a revolution, which police were duty-bound to foil at any cost. It was a catch-22 for honest men, a license to steal for the rest.

Reckford might go either way, as far as Bolan was concerned. Giving away a business card was no commitment. As for Quarrie's address—if it proved to be legitimate, and not a trap he'd thought up on the spot—the sergeant might begin to brood over his personal responsibility for what came next. Some cops could live with it, embittered by the filth they had to wade through every day, the predators they saw slip through the tattered net of justice. Others couldn't bear the strain. It would begin to gnaw at them, maybe invade their dreams.

With any luck, if Reckford went that way, Bolan would already be out of Kingston, safely Stateside. If not…well, it wouldn't be the first time Bolan waged his war against an underworld cartel while ducking cops at the same time. It made his work more difficult, but not impossible.

So time was of the essence. And what else was new?

Passing Kingston's Downtown Market, closed now, Bolan started watching for the turnoff onto Bustamante Highway, westbound. Once he made that turn, he'd be on the Viper Posse's home turf, penetrating Kingston's most notorious slum. He had a fix on Quarrie's hideout now, if such it was, from satellite images. The house was square, surrounded by a larger rectangle of grass and asphalt, likely fortified, although those renovations were invisible from space.

How many soldiers would the posse leader have surrounding him? There wasn't a number that would intimidate Bolan. He'd been facing long odds from the day he first put on his country's uniform, through all the long years of his private war. When he penetrated Quarrie's stronghold, he would be prepared for anything the enemy might throw at him, and give it back in kind.

That was life—and death—in Bolan's world. He did the best he could, in terms of preparation, then relied on strength, skill and audacity to do the rest. So far, that combination had been adequate to keep him breathing, keep him fighting. Friends helped, too, the team at Stony Man, but when it came to rolling up the enemy, he bore that burden on his own.

Three blocks, and Bolan started looking for a place to stash the Camry while he made his probe. The neighborhood was mostly residential, but he found a small convenience store half a block southwest of Quarrie's place. He stood beside the car in shadow, strapping on his gear, slinging the L85A1 rifle from his shoulder, underneath a lightweight raincoat.

Ready.

Staying in the dark as much as possible, he walked back toward the killing zone.

Port Kingston Causeway

IT WAS GOOD to leave Kingston behind him, rolling westward, with the city fading, blurring, in his rearview mirror. Quarrie felt himself beginning to relax already, even knowing that the struggle was not over and the worst might still be waiting for him. Movement, in and of itself, had healing qualities.

It wasn't really *running*, he'd convinced himself, but rather seeking an improved position on a mobile battle-field, from which to kill his enemy. Or to *evade* him. Either way, survival was the top priority, and he wasn't concerned with anyone who mistook his intentions.

Not yet, anyway.

He had a spliff going, surrounded by the heady smell of ganja, but he didn't share it with his men. He wanted them alert throughout their journey and upon arrival at his home away from home. It was unlikely that his foe could find the place before Quarrie arrived, but every-thing he'd suffered in the past few days had been unlikely. Near impossible, in fact.

The weapon in his lap—an Uzi submachine gun with a folding metal stock and 32-round magazine—was prob-ably unnecessary, with his well-armed soldiers all around, but who could say for sure? Even as mellow as he felt right now, the eight-pound weapon resting on his thighs provided comfort. Like the Kevlar vest he wore beneath his tailored jacket.

He might have worn a helmet if he'd had one, but the thought of squeezing one over his dreadlocks brought a smile to Quarrie's face. He nearly laughed aloud, in fact, but swallowed it with more smoke from the spliff.

His enemies, whoever they were, would expect him to stay hidden in the city. Quarrie thought—hoped—that the last place they would look for him was on a farm ten miles west of the capital, out beyond Portmore, south of Morris Meadows. His closest neighbors lived something like a quarter-mile from Quarrie's house, and they were private types who didn't welcome visitors or come snoop-ing around another's property without an invitation. If they knew who occupied the place from time to time, if they discussed it over rum or Red Stripe, they wouldn't share their conclusions with outsiders.

It was true he hadn't fortified the farmhouse, as he had the house in Tivoli Gardens. Certain renovations had made the place more comfortable and secure, but Quarrie hadn't gone all out. How could he have guessed it would ever come to this?

Ah, it'll be good enough, he thought, and hoped that was true. He had a dozen men already waiting for him, plus the soldiers in his caravan, and he'd put out the call for others to arrive as soon as possible. Not quite an army, but he thought it should be good enough to keep him breathing through the night.

Or was that the ganja talking?

Quarrie *did* laugh then, and saw a couple of his men shoot sidelong glances toward him, trying not to frown. He grinned at them and said, "Think about the fun we'll have if this bastard finds us after all."

12

Tivoli Gardens, Kingston

Bolan circled the property once more, on foot this time, and found his point of entry at the rear, a locked gate that faced an alley lined with garbage cans. The other fences, small garages, and what have you had been tagged with gang signs and more elaborate graffiti, but Quarrie's wall remained pristine, untouched by any of the slums artists.

Bolan thought of simply climbing over, then decided that could be a problem if he had to exit in a hurry. Instead, he drew the Glock 18, stepped back a pace, and fired a 3-round burst into the spot where the latch must be. The shots were nicely muffled, but their impact on the wood and latch were clearly audible, a short, harsh ripping sound. He waited in the darkness for a sentry to respond, then pushed his way in through the gate when no one came.

Swapping his pistol for the L85A1 rifle, Bolan clung to shadows as he worked his way around the sizable backyard. Someone had planted half a dozen trees in there, and they'd been growing long enough to reach a decent size, providing cover in the night as well as shade by day. With any luck, they'd get him almost to the back porch, unobserved.

Inside the house, lights burned in half a dozen rooms, at least. He saw a shadow pass one window. With the blinds pulled down, there was no way to tell if whomever he'd seen was armed. If he expected the worst, as usual, he would have the best chance of surviving what came next.

Closer, he noted that the windows with their blinds up were protected by thick screens *inside* the house. He'd seen that kind of thing before, with people who were fearful of grenades and IEDs lobbed from outside. It told him someone had put thought into protecting Quarrie's hideaway, but he still wondered why they hadn't stationed any men in the backyard.

As if in answer to his thought, the back door opened, spilling light on the porch, as a young man emerged. He wore the Rasta hat and baggy shirt that Bolan knew were *de rigueur* for posse soldiers, and he had some version of an AK-47 slung across his body on a shoulder strap. He seemed to have no sense of danger lurking in the nearby shadows, barely looked around the yard at all before he turned to shut the door behind him.

Bolan rushed the porch, Glock drawn and ready, squeezing off a single silent round that knocked the sentry's knitted beanie out of shape and turned his legs to rubber. Bolan caught him as he fell, one handed, covering the open doorway with his pistol as he eased the dead man down onto the porch. He waited for someone to call out, ask what the noise was, but it passed unnoticed.

Switching guns again, he stepped around the corpse and went inside.

BUSTER BAILEY HATED being left behind, even though he'd been left in charge. The boss had run away, his second in command was dead, so what did that make Bailey, after all? Was he a trusted officer, or just a decoy for the white man who'd been ripping the posse a new one all night long?

"Just my fortune," Bailey muttered to himself. Bad luck and nothing more. He'd been the highest-ranking

soldier left when Quarrie finished picking out his bodyguards, and that was how it happened. There'd been no
great thought invested into choosing someone suitable.

Just someone Quarrie thought he could afford to lose.

Bailey kept moving through the house, from room to
room. All the outer walls were reinforced with sandbags
to the level of the lowest windows, and mattresses were
fastened higher up with wire and nails. Some heavy slugs
would penetrate regardless, but at least the padding on the
inside of the walls would slow them down. Screens on
the windows would block tear gas canisters or anything
attackers threw by hand, except homemade incendiar-
ies, and each window had at least one fire extinguisher
standing nearby.

Beyond that, if the enemy brought RPGs or flame-
throwers, maybe a tank, then it was over. But you'd go
down fighting, bet your life on that, and take some of the
bastards with you.

"I don't plan to die tonight," he told himself, half whis-
pering, as he went to check the kitchen, make sure nobody was in there stuffing his face when he should be on
watch. No one was there, and Bailey suddenly felt hungry, standing in the room alone, with the refrigerator and
the cupboards full of food.

He thought about corned beef and butter beans, knew
he could empty out a couple cans and put their contents
in the microwave. Could almost taste it now.

If someone else came in, he'd tell them to shove off
and—

When the first shots came, they made him flinch. Bailey spun toward the sound, lifting his AK-101, leaving its
stock folded against the left side of the rifle's receiver. He
didn't shout to find out what was happening, preferred
surprise if there were enemies inside the house, and not
just some idiot who was careless with his weapon.

When he reached the kitchen door, Bailey leaned out to look both ways, saw no one in the corridor, and stepped clear of the entryway. The shots, he thought, had come from somewhere to the right of where he stood, and shouting from the same direction tended to confirm it. Swallowing an urge to run out through the back door and escape, he moved off toward the angry voices.

"Who's that shootin'?" someone called out.

"I don't know," someone else replied. "Some crazy brother."

"Where'd it come from?"

"Somewhere in the back."

"Maybe the playroom."

Bailey could have shouted at them to be quiet, but he didn't want to draw attention to himself just yet. Someone might react instinctively and cut him down before they realized who'd spoken, giving orders in the midst of chaos.

"Goddamn idiots!" he snarled, slowing his pace as he drew closer to the playroom—not a child's place, but a recreation area with arcade games, a sixty-five-inch flat-screen television, and a DVD collection running heavily toward porn.

A few more yards and he was almost there, when an explosion rocked the house and loosed a rain of plaster on his head.

BOLAN HADN'T PLANNED to use a frag grenade so soon, but it was unavoidable. He'd only been inside the house for thirty seconds, give or take, just time to get a feel for how the place was fortified, when he'd met a Rasta soldier in a spacious room resembling a video arcade. No one was on the games when he walked in, but one of Quarrie's men was setting up a movie in a DVD player, smoking a joint to prove he could multitask. The guy saw Bolan when he straightened up and lost the doobie when his mouth dropped open.

His next move was reaching for a pistol underneath his T-shirt, but he never grasped the weapon. Bolan let his L85A1 speak for him, putting one 5.56 mm NATO round through the gunman's forehead and slamming him backward into a humongous flat-screen TV. It toppled with him, crashing to the floor as people started shouting back and forth from other rooms.

So much for stealth.

He'd known there would be fighting, but he'd also hoped he might get close to Quarrie first—or see him, at the very least—before it hit the fan. Now Bolan didn't even know if his intended prey was in the house.

A bad start, and the worst was yet to come.

He turned to leave the game room, just as two more Rasta shooters reached the doorway, stopping short and hoisting weapons toward the enemy in their midst. Bolan shot one of them, a clean hit to the upper chest, before his partner ducked back out of sight and started calling for assistance, no doubt covering the exit. In another moment, he heard reinforcements moving up to join the fight, all shouting at each other, some of them cocking weapons.

That was when he reached for the grenade, released its pin and pitched the green egg through the open doorway, ducking behind a sofa sectional before it blew. There were no mattresses or sandbags stacked against the room's dividing walls to stop shrapnel from slicing through, no soundproofing to muffle anguished cries of pain.

He went among them then, before the dust and smoke cleared, found two of four soldiers still moving, and gave each a round through the head as he passed. Deeper into the fortified house, beyond his line of sight, men were shouting and feet were scrambling, Quarrie's soldiers responding to the sounds of battle. Bolan sleeved plaster dust from his forehead and moved on to meet them.

He could end it here, if luck was with him—or if it deserted him. Whichever outcome lay in store, he was prepared.

A pistol shot rang out ahead of Bolan, bullet whining past his head to strike a nearby wall. He ducked as other weapons joined the chorus, shooters firing blindly through the haze of dust and smoke that filled the hallway, hoping for a lucky hit. Rather than risk a stray shot drilling him, Bolan dropped prone and started crawling forward, powered by his knees and elbows, moving steadily in the direction of his enemies.

BUSTER BAILEY HUDDLED with a small clutch of his soldiers, roughly one-third of the men Quarrie had left to guard his house in Tivoli, and hissed at them, "Do you see him? Where is he?"

"I can't see anything," one of them whispered back. "Maybe we got him."

"I'll believe that when I see him dead," Bailey replied. "Somebody needs to go find out."

"Who's going then?" asked another man.

"You and you," Bailey replied, nudging the last man who'd spoken and the fellow next to him.

"Why should I go?" the second man demanded.

"'Cause I said so," Bailey snapped at him, bringing his AK-101's muzzle to bear on the uneasy soldier. "You want to argue with me?"

Both men glared at Bailey for a moment, then one shook his head. The other muttered, "No," and started creeping forward on all fours, along the hallway where their enemy had last revealed himself. The rounds they'd fired in his direction had released more dust from the walls and ceiling, likely without doing any good, and Bailey meant to put it right.

But he was not about to take the lead. No way.

Bailey hadn't fired a shot yet, so his rifle's magazine was brimming full with thirty 5.56 mm rounds. He craved an opportunity to fire them all at once, riddling his enemy from head to toe, reducing him to raw hamburger where he stood, but so far there'd been no opening.

How many Rastas had the prowler killed? It was impossible to say without a final head count, and the present circumstances rendered that impossible. If they could stop him quick enough, then sweep the place before the beasts of Babylon arrived, he would be able to tell Quarrie what had happened. Give him some good news.

But otherwise…

Being arrested in a house with corpses, automatic weapons and other assorted evidence of criminal activity could finish him. The Viper Posse might have friends in government, even at court, but "aggravated" murder was a capital crime in Jamaica. Recovery of drugs and weapons from the house meant long terms of imprisonment, even if Bailey's lawyer managed to convince a jury that he'd injured no one personally. Getting out was still his best bet, but too many men had seen him at the forefront of the fight. If he ran now, and word got back to Quarrie, he could wind up on a makeshift altar with his heart cut out and a *papaloi* sipping his blood.

He'd nearly lost sight of his point men now, nearing a corner of the hallway, hesitating there. "Go on!" he urged them, without knowing whether they could hear him. While gunfire had ceased within the house, for now, his ears still rang from the explosion moments earlier.

His men had reached the corner now, and were conferring there before they made their next move. Bailey saw one rise up to a crouch, duck-walking toward the turn, wobbling as he tried to keep a firm grip on his automatic rifle. Finally, he lurched up and stagger-charged around the corner, shouting, "Fire for you!" and squeezing off a long, wild burst.

Bailey didn't hear the responding shot that dropped his man and sent the other scuttling backward, seeking cover. "Get back there and catch up!" he ordered, shouting it. His soldier hesitated, weighing options for a second, then turned back and started crawling toward the body of his fallen friend.

SOMEONE HAD TAKEN CHARGE, was giving orders now, and Bolan had to figure at least some of the posse soldiers would obey them. He'd left a trail of dead behind him, but he still had no idea how many enemies remained in fighting shape, or where he would find Quarrie in the urban bunker.

If he was there at all.

The only way to find out now was to defeat the force that still opposed him, try to capture one of them alive and capable of speaking, squeeze him for a simple answer to a simple question, maybe two or three, before police arrived.

So, do it!

Bolan palmed another frag grenade and primed it, clutched it in his left hand as he surged around the corner, bullpup rifle firm and steady in his right. He caught one of the shooters who'd been creeping up on him, his comrades farther down the hallway urging him along. Bolan triggered a 3-round burst that took most of the creeping gunman's head off, then released his L109A1 high-explosive egg, making an overhanded pitch downrange.

And hit the floor again, before it blew.

The *wham* of the explosion stung his ears, no way around that, but he rode it out and waited for the screams to follow. Moved in when they started, finding one man nearly dead and three more down with shrapnel wounds of varying severity. One had his hands clamped over ringing ears, but should have paid attention to the bright blood pumping out of his femoral artery.

Bolan had no way to determine which of them had been in charge before the blast. He grabbed one, gave his neck a painful twist and asked, "Where's Quarrie?"

"He's gone, white man," came the answer.

"Gone where?"

"To visit yo mama."

Bolan's rifle butt cracked against the man's skull. He grabbed another moaning Rasta and repeated his inquiry. "Where did Quarrie go?"

The wounded soldier saw death in his eyes and answered, "He's got a special place, outside of Portmore."

"*Where* by Portmore?"

"West of there, and south of Morris Meadows."

"Give me an address!"

"Don't know it. Only know the way to drive there."

"Never mind," Bolan replied, and let him slump back to the floor. He heard a siren in the distance, and imagined that the gunfire might have drawn a crowd outside, which might prove hostile to a pale-faced stranger fleeing Quarrie's home. His time was running out.

No one tried to impede him as he cleared the killing ground, out through the back door and across the yard, the gate still standing open for him. Two uneasy-looking neighbors stood in the alley, but the sight of Bolan's weapons easily dissuaded them from whatever action they might have considered. He was at the Camry's wheel and out of there before the first cruiser came screeching to a halt on Bustamante Highway.

And his Quarrie had eluded him once more.

The wounded posse gunman hadn't seemed like he was

lying, but there were no guarantees. He'd have to check it out, and if he didn't find his man, come back to Kingston for another try.

Fortunes of war, and Bolan wasn't giving up.

Slipe Road, Kingston

SERGEANT CLANCY RECKFORD was en route to Tivoli Gardens when a radio call diverted him northward, to Oxford Road and the Ministry of National Security. Undersecretary Perry Campbell required his presence without delay, although the JCF dispatcher couldn't tell him what the reason was.

Another interruption. More bad news.

Cursing, Reckford did as he was told, traveling the mile or so to his unwelcome destination while his mind raced, trying to decipher why he'd been summoned. Had someone observed him with the white man and reported it? If so, who could it be? And how on earth could the report have reached a bureaucrat as highly placed as Campbell in the half hour since he'd left the diner with his breakfast barely touched?

The summons was unprecedented. Campbell would normally speak to the JCF's commissioner, his deputy, or one of the force's senior superintendents. In special cases—if a wealthy tourist had been murdered, or an act of terrorism was committed—Campbell might hear details from the lead detectives, for the benefit of his superiors. He had no personal investigative function, was a paper-pusher and a politician, not a law-enforcement officer.

So, *why*?

Reckford tuned his dashboard radio to Irie FM, hoping some reggae would relax him, but it had the opposite effect, making him think about the Viper Posse and the white man who was hell-bent on destroying them. A part of Reckford wished him luck; another part regretted not arresting him while they were face-to-face—assuming he could have managed it.

Reckford left his car in the ministry's parking lot, went inside and rode the elevator up to Campbell's office. There was no receptionist at that hour, but he found the waiting room unlocked and entered, calling Campbell's name. Another moment passed before the man himself emerged and curtly ordered Reckford, "Follow me."

The undersecretary's private office was luxurious enough, but not as posh as Reckford had imagined. He sat facing Campbell, with a good-size maple desk between them, Campbell peering at him as if Reckford were a member of some species he couldn't quite recognize.

"You know why I called you here?" he asked, at last.

"No, sir."

"No? I should have thought it would be obvious."

"I was dispatched here, sir. That's all I know."

"You are the lead investigator in the recent spate of murders, here in Kingston."

Was he? Cautious, Reckford answered, "Under supervision of my captain and lieutenant, sir."

"And are they satisfied with your performance?"

"I've heard nothing to the contrary." He dropped the *sir* this time.

"Indeed? Have you made *any* progress?"

"I am pursuing leads as usual, and—"

"Did you say 'as usual'?"

"Yes, sir."

"With two outstanding citizens already dead?"

"To whom are you referring, sir?"

"Henry Boothe and Aaron Moncrief," Campbell answered. "Who else would I mean?"

"I have no way of knowing, sir. You realize they were agents of the Viper Posse?"

"That is hearsay, very likely slanderous! You will take special care to keep all such opinions to yourself. If I should see them in the press, or hear them on the television—"

"They will not have come from me, sir."

"Are you normally this insubordinate?"

"Sir?"

"When I give an order, I expect it to be followed!"

"I've received no orders from your office, sir."

"Oh, no? Then take *this* as my order. You shall instantly desist from all harassment of the city's leading businessmen. Is that clear, Sergeant?"

"No, sir. Did you have specific businessmen in mind?"

"I think you know exactly who I mean." He was afraid to say it openly.

"And if they are potential victims, possibly with knowledge of the people who may wish to harm them, am I barred from speaking to them?"

"You will leave interrogation of your betters to the ministry."

"With all respect, sir, that makes my position rather difficult."

"I'll solve that problem for you. As of now, you are suspended for two weeks—with pay, unless you wish to argue further?"

"No, sir. Thank you, sir. If that is all…?"

"It is. Dismissed."

Reckford felt dizzy as he left the office, walked back to the elevator, headed down and out into the night. He still had no idea exactly what had happened, much less *why*. Someone was pulling strings to stifle the investiga-

tion, or to lead it down a certain avenue, and part of Reckford's mind thought he was well rid of the thankless task.
Another part, however, told him he couldn't let it go.

13

Saint Catherine Parish, Jamaica

From the Port Kingston Causeway, Quarrie's caravan rolled north, following Dyke Road until the lead car reached Passage Fort Drive and turned inland. At Municipal Boulevard, the small procession crossed onto Grange Lane. Halfway to Morris Meadows they turned south once again, onto a nameless access road. Another twenty minutes, give or take, and they'd reached their destination.

Quarrie's driver called ahead, alerting the defenders on the property. Surprising them would be a bad idea, considering the state of high alert they'd maintained since trouble started back in Kingston. A shootout with his own men was the last thing Quarrie needed at the moment.

Guards at the entrance to the property saluted Quarrie as he passed, all armed with automatic weapons openly displayed.

On arrival at the farmhouse, Quarrie was relieved to stretch his legs. The man in charge of his retreat, Asafa Tulloch, greeted Quarrie with a double handshake, saying, "Glad you made it, Boss."

"Is he here?" Quarrie inquired.

"Ready and waiting for you."

Quarrie turned away from Tulloch, left him standing with the bodyguards from Kingston, and proceeded toward a bungalow that stood apart from other buildings in the compound, with fifty yards of empty ground on every side. Arriving at the door, he opened it without a warning knock and stepped inside.

Usain Dalhouse, the *papaloi*, rose from a metal folding chair as Quarrie entered, face deadpan. The white shirt he wore over a pair of khaki trousers was pristine, so far. His tools were laid out on a card table behind him, placed so that the sacrificial lamb could see them.

Quarrie didn't ask where Dalhouse had obtained the child, or how. It was irrelevant. After their sacrifice in Kingston had failed to conjure the desired result, Dalhouse had said a stronger message to the gods might be required. Blood of the young and innocent was far more potent than an adult's. Their unmitigated suffering demanded full attention on the Other Side.

Quarrie had no idea what he was paying for the child— a little girl—nor did he care. Results were all that mattered. He'd informed Dalhouse in no uncertain terms that failure, this time, meant he would be next under the knife. Yet here he was, no sign of trepidation on his face or in his manner.

Quarrie dispensed with greetings. Asked his servant, "Do we do it all the same?"

"The more time you can spare, the better," Dalhouse answered.

Quarrie moved to stand over the child, bound to a table like the ones so often seen in cafeterias. She'd been crying and started up again as she stared into his eyes.

"No drugs this time?"

"She must feel all of it," Dalhouse replied.

Quarrie stood waiting for the idea to repulse him, but it didn't happen. He had come prepared for this, and now found he was looking forward to it.

If the gods would not assist him after this, to hell with them.

"All right," he said. "Where do I start?"

Portmore, Jamaica

BOLAN WAS PASSING one of the island's Seventh-Day Adventist Churches when he tried Clancy Reckford's cell number. The phone rang twice, was starting on its third time, when the sergeant answered.

"What?"

"How was the ackee?" Bolan asked.

"You killed my appetite."

"Sorry to hear it," Bolan said. "How's your investigation going?"

"It goes on without me," Reckford answered. "I've been suspended."

Frowning, Bolan asked him, "Why?"

"There was no explanation, only orders."

"Well," Bolan said thoughtfully, "maybe you're best left out of it, at that."

"Left out of what?"

"The finish. Quarrie's gone to ground outside of Portmore, on some kind of ranch or farm."

"I know the place."

He took a chance. "I'm nearly there, and I'd appreciate it if you wouldn't tip off your people that I'm coming."

There was bitterness in Reckford's tone as he replied, "I have no people any longer."

"Hey, suspended's not the same as fired."

"It means I'm superfluous. They don't need me. Now, I wonder whether I need them."

Bolan wasn't a counselor. He didn't normally do pep talks and wasn't inclined to give one now. Reckford could deal with his own problems, didn't need a total stranger butting in. "Good thing you're out of it. Take care," he said, and cut the link.

If Reckford didn't contact the constables in Portmore, they'd have to get their first news of the rain from any neighbors Quarrie had. The satellite view showed a broad expanse of wooded land, trees covering the northern and the western flanks of Quarrie's spread. Its entrance, on the east side, faced a narrow access road. Southward lay open fields, which might be under cultivation with some crop he couldn't recognize from space.

He'd catch the access road from Portmore, passing by the city's police station, noted on his cyber-map as a hundred-man facility. The longer he could leave those coppers out of any action, the better he would like it, and the greater Bolan's chances of escape, when he was done.

If he was still alive.

Defeatism was alien to Bolan's nature. He examined problems as they came, prepared himself to deal with them as fully as he could, then did his best. So far, his best had been enough.

Tonight? He'd have to wait and see.

Saint Catherine Parish

DALE HOLBROOK HAD driven from Kingston with his Glock 22 on the passenger's seat, ready for a quick grab if he ran into trouble. He'd have to tuck the piece away, though, so it didn't rattle Quarrie's bodyguards.

Conceal it, right. But he'd be damned if anyone was taking it away from him.

He counted this night wasted, and he'd have trouble trying to explain it if anyone at the embassy pressed him. They'd been cool so far, pretending not to know his true function, but the ambassador herself might have some questions for him if she learned that he'd stayed out all night, doing God knows what. Holbrook's link to the Viper Posse was strictly need-to-know, and in Langley's view, *nobody* needed to know besides a few guys at head-quarters.

And the director, of course. He knew and *didn't* know, the way he liked to keep it with their down-and-dirty games. A little dose of plausible deniability.

So Holbrook would be short on sleep, holding a gangster's hand all night, trying to reassure him that he'd still be safe tomorrow. He'd tell Quarrie they were getting somewhere with the search for his mysterious opponents, when the opposite was true. Holbrook still didn't have a clue whom they were looking for.

No problem. Lying was his stock in trade, a staple of the Company. Holbrook had lied to everybody he could think of since he took this job, from family and confidential informants, on up the chain of command to his bosses. Real life, he'd found, was a lot like that Don Henley song "Dirty Laundry." Most people really didn't want to know what was going on behind the scenes, much less how far it had gone.

The access road was narrow, flanked by trees and shadows on both sides. He passed one dark house before his GPS told him he was close to Quarrie's gate. Slowing almost to a stop, he took the Glock, slipped it underneath his belt in back and made sure it was secure before proceeding.

There were gunmen on the gate, no big surprise. They flagged him down, got close and peered inside the car with flashlights, made him pop the trunk to make sure he didn't have a bomb or tiny ninjas tucked away back there. One of them walkie-talkied to the farmhouse, getting clearance for him to proceed. They both looked vaguely disappointed when they didn't have to shoot him.

Animals.

Dealing with scumbags was a fact of Holbrook's life, and while he'd gotten used to it, that didn't translate into *liking* it. Given his druthers, he'd have mowed them down en masse—or, at the very least, imprisoned them and thrown away the keys—but this was real life, not some rosy fantasy.

He drove up to the house, remembering his way from last time. More riflemen were waiting for him there, one of them showing Holbrook where to park his car. They didn't try to frisk him when he stepped out, which was something, but they clearly weren't inclined to let him stroll around the compound, either.

"Boss is comin' in a minute," one informed him. "We wait here."

Holbrook nodded, saw no need to comment on the order. While he waited, leaning back against the fender of his ride, he took stock of the place. It was an armed camp, not at all the laid-back getaway he remembered from his last visit. It didn't take a general to know that Quarrie was at war, preparing for what might be his last stand.

The "minute" had run into five and counting when he saw Quarrie emerging from a bungalow, some fifty yards due west of where the guards were keeping Holbrook. Shirtless, the posse boss approached. Strange white marks were visible across his chest and abdomen, some kind of body paint. And if that wasn't weird enough, his face and upper chest were also smeared with blood.

"Ah good, you're here," Quarrie said, all the greeting he could muster. "We have lots to talk about."

Holbrook was prepared to shake his hand, but Quarrie held back, raising both of his, all dripping red. "I need to shower first. Come on with me and have a drink."

Resigned to ask nothing about the blood, Holbrook fell into step beside his host, moving through semidarkness toward the house.

BOLAN KILLED THE CAMRY'S headlights as he turned onto a smaller unpaved road and made his way west, overshadowed by tall trees on either side. He trusted the odometer to tell him when he'd driven far enough, then started looking for a place to hide the car.

Not easy, in the present circumstances, but he found *another* access lane, this one running north-south, and swung into it, killing the Toyota's engine. There'd been no sign of human activity since he'd cleared Portmore's suburbs, and Bolan thought the odds of someone passing by and discovering his ride were close to astronomical. Quarrie might have patrols out, working his perimeter, but Bolan was outside what anyone would think of as a normal range.

He changed clothes standing by the car, in the warm, humid night. His skintight blacksuit clung like thermal underwear, but without stifling him. Over the outfit went his shoulder rig and web gear, weapons and spare magazines, the Chaos trench knife in its sheath at Bolan's waist. He took both rifles with him, just in case, but thought the AS50 likely wouldn't do him much good.

The half-mile hike to Quarrie's spread would take some time and care. He'd be approaching from the northeast, coming through the trees and taking full advantage of them. Moving quietly through any forest was a challenge, all the more so when your enemies were on alert to any false step, any sound they hadn't heard a thousand times before.

One of his specialties.

Rollington Town, Jamaica

"Suspended, am I?" Clancy Reckford muttered as he packed his gear. "To hell with that! To hell with you!"

Nobody was there to hear him. Perry Campbell was far away in his posh condominium, likely dozing through the night's last hours while Reckford hastily prepared for war. He'd switched his Browning pistol to a shoulder holster that he rarely wore, twin pouches underneath his right arm holding two spare magazines. Four more lay inside an old gym bag, ready for transfer to his pockets when he got to Quarrie's country place. His little secret—not so little, maybe not so secret—was an MP5A3 machine pistol and six 30-round magazines. Both weapons fired the same 9 mm Parabellum ammunition, and he'd placed two spare boxes of cartridges into the gym bag, as well.

Not that he believed there'd be time to reload, once the killing began.

He placed his submachine gun in the gym bag with the extra ammunition, zipped it up and slung the strap over his shoulder. It was heavy with the weight of a decision made that could not be reversed. Whatever happened in the next few hours, prior to dawn, it meant a drastic change in life as Reckford knew it.

Probably the end of his career. Perhaps the end of life itself.

And would that be so bad? He was unmarried, with no prospects for a wife and family. He'd soured on his job, watching the officers around him and the higher-ups who ruled them breaking all the laws they'd sworn to uphold and defend. Reckford himself was not an angel, but he'd never taken bribes to look the other way. Had never sold his soul.

Clearly, he was the odd man out, incapable of changing the others. If he died tonight they wouldn't miss him. But if he survived…then, what?

Retaliation from the Viper Posse? From the Ministry of National Security? He'd made an enemy of Perry Campbell as it was, and what he planned to do might well land him in prison, if he lived to face the charges.

Downstairs, Reckford climbed into the vehicle he'd borrowed from headquarters without sanction, one of thirty-nine Mitsubishi L200 4X4 pickups purchased by the JCF last autumn. This one was unmarked but had a siren, flashing lights behind its grille and on the rear windowsill, together with a shotgun mounted in a dashboard rack immediately to his left.

Reckford gunned the engine and squealed away from the curb, heading toward Portmore. He had the two-way radio turned on, listened for any calls that might pertain to him as he ate up the miles, leaving the city lights behind.

Saint Catherine Parish

BOLAN MET THE FIRST sentry a hundred yards out from Quarrie's compound. The man was on patrol, or was supposed to be, but he'd stopped to rest, slouching against a tree and smoking something that didn't smell like tobacco. The soldier was already tired of his part in the game, and that laziness was about to cost him his life.

Bolan unsheathed the Chaos trench knife, creeping up behind his man, using the night for cover until he had closed to striking range. A quick punch then, slamming the knife's notched knuckle guard into the Rasta's face, crushing the bone around one eye. He started dropping, sliding down the tree, and met the black blade as it rose, 7.5 inches of double-edged steel piercing under his chin and up through the soft palate to silence all thought. A warm rush of blood over Bolan's right hand, and the job was finished.

He eased the body down, wiped his knife and hand on the lookout's loose shirt, then unloaded the man's Kalashnikov, tossing its magazine into the night. A frisk for the pistol, repeating the procedure, and he left the corpse unarmed, in case somebody came along and tried to use the weapons to his disadvantage later.

Moving closer to his target, Bolan started watching out for booby traps, as well as sentries. Grenades with trip wires, possibly, or something more primitive: pitfalls or deadfalls, snares or crude javelins launched by the spring of bent saplings. Bolan had seen and survived it all in his time, but it never paid to be careless.

Overconfidence kills.

At sixty yards he saw the first lights from the compound, through the trees. Instead of hurrying, he slowed his pace, knowing the risks increased as he drew closer to the kill zone. He could hear a good-size generator running, powering the lights and various appliances. An air conditioner kicked in, cooling the house.

He thought about communications, figured they'd have cells and sat-phones, maybe two-way radios as well, but none of it would help them now. It didn't matter if the Rastas called for reinforcements once the action started. By the time fresh faces could arrive from Portmore, much less Kingston, they would be too late. The battle would be over, one way or another.

Edging closer to the lights, he hunkered down beneath a tree. He scanned the house and outbuildings, the open space between them, marking sentries on patrol and other men who drifted here and there at random—to a bunkhouse, off to the latrine, or toward a lighted building that he thought must be a mess hall, from the odors it produced. The night was winding down, but some of them were still on duty, others just too wired to sleep.

How many?

Bolan couldn't tell but guessed there must be more inside the house, and in the bunkhouse, sleeping. All of them would scramble when the shooting started, focused on the goal of killing him.

But they'd have to spot him first.

14

Asafa Tulloch stepped out of the farmhouse kitchen into shadows. Lights hadn't been placed throughout the compound, since his boss feared drawing unwanted attention, particularly from the air. The buildings were illuminated, and a light pole stood on its own near the barn. Beyond those pools of luminescence, you could walk for thirty yards or more in almost total darkness.

Ample room to sneak a spliff, to keep him mellow.

First, though, Tulloch had a job to do, checking the sentries, making sure *they* weren't too mellow. Most of those he'd picked were walking beats around the site's perimeter, but there were two on duty at the entrance to the farmhouse, two more cleaning up after the boss's sacrifice.

That was a filthy job, but someone had to do it, or the mess drew flies. Tulloch had done the job himself, once, and had never managed to forget it. He'd been confused at first, over the dabbling in Obeah when they were supposed to be loyal Rastafari, worshipping Haile Selassie, but he hadn't let it trouble him for long. Mayhem was part of Tulloch's world, and if a little mutilation gave the boss man peace—or cowed his enemies and made them easier to kill—so be it. Tulloch had no problem playing along.

He was about to roust a soldier smoking near the tree line, maybe take the spliff away from him and keep it for himself, when a gunshot cracked out behind him. Tulloch spun to face the motor pool, where he believed the sound had come from, just in time to see one of his sentries breaking from the shadows, turning back to raise his rifle, aiming somewhere into the night. He may have been the one who'd fired, but he didn't get a chance to try again. A muzzle-flash winked from the shadows in between a four-door pickup and an SUV, the short burst knocking Tulloch's man flat on his back.

"Intruders!" Tulloch bellowed. "Wake up and fetch your weapons!"

Tulloch slipped his own Barrett REC7 assault rifle off its shoulder sling and cocked it in one fluid motion. Already moving toward the motor pool, Tulloch called out again, "Get your weapons!"

And the words had barely left his mouth before he saw the enemy—or one of them, at least—emerging from the shadows where he'd glimpsed the deadly muzzle-flash a moment earlier. He was a tall man, definitely white, though dressed in black to camouflage himself. He carried some kind of assault rifle Tulloch didn't recognize, along with other weapons strapped around him, high and low.

Go for it! Tulloch thought, and snapped the Barrett to his shoulder, aiming through its holographic sight. He pegged the red dot on his target's chest from sixty yards, his index finger curled around the rifle's trigger, and he squeezed—just as the white man ducked and dodged away.

His bullet struck the four-door pickup, drilling through its left-front fender, finishing its flight somewhere inside the engine compartment. Tulloch lifted off the rifle's sight, scanning the motor pool for any sign of his intended target, and saw nothing.

"Where in hell did he go?" he asked himself.

And rushed to find the man who'd disappeared.

BOLAN HAD SEEN the red dot dancing on his chest in time to drop and roll beneath the pickup to his right. He was covered when the bullet struck the vehicle above him with a *clang* and spent its force against the engine block, starting a steady drip of gasoline where it had clipped the fuel line.

He was out from under the pickup, crouching on the driver's side, a pair of motorcycles at his back, before his would-be killer closed in on the motor pool, calling to others for assistance. "Come here!" he barked. "I've got him over here!"

No one answered, but a peek around the pickup's right-front fender told him others were responding silently, running to join the rifleman who'd almost reached his destination now. Bolan decided on the spot that it made more sense to distract them than engage them in a skirmish where he might well be pinned down.

He plucked a frag grenade from his belt, pulled the pin and rolled the bomb into the puddle of gasoline spreading beneath the pickup's front end. Four seconds to evacuate, and Bolan used them to his best advantage, hurdling the nearest motorcycle, sliding across the hood of an SUV painted in camouflage, and dropping out of sight before the world caught fire.

The blast lifted the pickup in a semblance of a wheelie, riding on a fireball underneath its engine and front axle. Shrapnel finished off the fuel line, pouring gasoline into the flames, and Bolan stayed low, waiting for the secondary detonation when its gas tank blew. He heard a scream in there, maybe the guy who'd tried to snipe him, then the other Rasta soldiers were shouting and rushing forward, searching for whoever was responsible for the explosion.

Bolan met them halfway, rising from behind the camo SUV and firing short, precision bursts to take them down. He counted four of them—the jumpy sentry who'd fired on him and missed made five. He couldn't guarantee that all of them were dead before they hit the ground, but they were on their way.

He left the flames behind him as another vehicle caught fire. Instead of running into trouble with the orange light at his back, he circled to his right and headed for the bungalow he'd spotted earlier, set off from Quarrie's house and barn as if the place demanded special privacy. No cables fed it electricity. There were no windows to reveal what lay inside.

He reached it, tried the door, and felt the knob turn in his hand. Palming a pencil flash, he slipped inside and played its beam around the structure's single room, the light showing him rusty bloodstains on a table at the center, on the floor, the walls, even the ceiling. Someone had been busy here. Whomever they had butchered had been living when it started.

Snarling silently, Bolan retreated to the door he'd left ajar, checked hurriedly for any danger on the threshold, and went out to find the man responsible.

DALE HOLBROOK CURSED himself for coming like a dog when Quarrie whistled for him. Now, with vehicles aflame and more exploding, gunfire hammering across the compound, he wished that he was anywhere except trapped between a gang of Rasta maniacs and someone bent on killing them.

Too late.

The time to second-guess his move had been when he was safe and comfy at the embassy. Now, huddled next to Quarrie and some other creepy asshole in the gangster's farmhouse, lights out, peering through a window at the chaos in the yard, he figured it was time to do or die.

"Who is this bastard?" Quarrie muttered, staring at the fires and muzzle-flashes lighting up his so-called hardsite. Next to him, the nameless creepy guy said nothing.

"You think one man's doing all that?" Holbrook asked. "Seriously?"

"One is all my people saw each time he hit us."

"So, they were confused," Holbrook replied. "The few that lived."

Truth was, he didn't care how many men were out there raising hell. If it were only one, that helped his odds of getting out alive, but only marginally. At the moment, Holbrook thought he was as likely to be shot by one of Quarrie's men as any outsider.

This wasn't Holbrook's thing. He'd passed the necessary courses, sure: firearms and demolition, unarmed self-defense, but no one would mistake him for a soldier. He'd come to the Company straight out of college, gung-ho as hell and hoping for adventure, ultimately satisfied to let civilian assets risk their asses while he sat behind a desk or met with them occasionally, safe as he could make himself with his credentials and his diplomatic license plates.

Now he was in the shit and there was no way out, other than getting dirty.

Could he kill a man? Holbrook had never doubted it before, in theory, gassing with his buddies over drinks, but now it didn't look so easy. This wasn't a hypothetical problem: What do you do when you find out an asset's betrayed you, or somebody's hot on your trail at the end of a covert meeting?

This was wholesale slaughter, and it terrified him.

A bullet drilled the windowpane above him, making Holbrook gasp, recoil and shame himself. Quarrie glanced over at him, bright shards in his dreadlocks glinting firelight, and regarded him with vague disdain.

"I'm going out there. Are you coming, or staying here to wet yourself?"

You're damn right I'm coming, Holbrook thought. And first chance I see, I'm getting out of here. But what he said, tight-lipped, was, "Lead the way."

"I'll make a man out of you yet," Quarrie said, flashing

him a grimace. Hefting his rifle—some kind of Kalashnikov, who knew the difference?—the gangster duckwalked to the door, reached up to turn the knob, then lunged into the night.

Holbrook was on his heels, sticking close on the assumption that proximity to Quarrie would at least protect him from the Rastas firing every which way. He assumed—hoped—they wouldn't shoot their boss, or anyone accompanying him. As for the raiders, while he realized that sticking close to Quarrie might be detrimental, Holbrook didn't plan to keep the mob boss company all night.

As soon as he could reach his car or find another working set of wheels, Holbrook would be gone so fast he'd leave this posse choking on his dust. The embassy could bill him for the car he'd borrowed, if they wanted to, or charge it to the Company.

He planned to stay alive, as Malcolm X once said, by any means necessary.

And then, thinking of how it had worked out for Malcolm, Holbrook suddenly felt sick with fear.

BOLAN DIDN'T KNOW what Quarrie prayed for in his grisly rituals, but it was safe to say he hadn't got his money's worth tonight. His soldiers were in disarray, most of his rolling stock had been consumed by fire or soon would be, and all the corpses strewn around the grounds so far were members of the home team. Plenty more were still in fighting trim, but they were frightened and disorganized, running around like chickens who'd lost their heads or were about to.

Bolan knew his best bet for a shot at Quarrie was the farmhouse. No one on the yard had managed to exert even a semblance of authority so far, which told him the boss was lying low. Biding his time, most likely, waiting till he had a clear view of his enemy—or else, a clear way out.

There would be other vehicles around the farm, outside the burning motor pool. Bolan could see a couple of them now. In the slaughter shed behind him, firelight glinted off chrome and metalwork where four-wheel drives and off-road bikes were parked at random.

One of the dreads came rushing at him from the shadows to his left, might have succeeded if he hadn't felt the need to howl his rage at the last second—or if he'd found a firearm to replace the cane knife he aimed at Bolan's skull. Bolan dropped underneath the roundhouse swing and whipped his rifle's butt around, changing the landscape of his adversary's face. The guy lurched backward, gasping now instead of shouting, lost his balance and sat down. A slug from Bolan's L85A1 punched through his forehead, fired at point-blank range, and made sure he didn't rise again.

No zombies here.

A swarm of bullets crackled past his face and Bolan hit the deck, rolling away to spoil the shooter's aim. He wound up facing toward the nearest sound of gunfire, looking at two of Quarrie's men who seemed amazed to find him still alive. Before they could digest it and correct their target acquisition, Bolan shot the taller of them in the groin and sent him sprawling, not the cleanest hit he'd ever made, but still effective.

Number two was torn between running and claiming the prize. He chose glory and leveled his TEC-9 at Bolan, but he did it too late. Before he could trigger the kill shot, Bolan's 5.56 mm tumblers ripped into his chest and ended him, his body tipping over backward, dropping on his buddy's wounded lower half. That wrenched a scream out of the soldier who was still alive, though not exactly kicking, while the Executioner jumped up and moved away.

Still hunting Quarrie, in the midst of hell on earth.

CLANCY RECKFORD PARKED two hundred yards from Quarrie's gate and walked in, burdened with his little private arsenal. The shotgun had no sling, so he was carrying it, pistol holstered, machine pistol slung across his back where he could reach it easily, his pockets weighted down with extra magazines and twelve-gauge cartridges.

From what he heard ahead of him, he might need all of that, and more.

The gate was closed but presently unguarded. Reckford guessed the watchmen had been drawn away to join the fight now raging on the inside of the compound's fence, men running, shouting, firing, dying. For a moment he was tempted to wait outside and let them kill each other, then he thought about the stranger who'd brought him here, and cursed his luck.

He hadn't come this far to simply stand and watch.

Shifting to one side of the gate, he leaped and placed his shotgun flat atop the eight-foot wall. A second leap, and Reckford caught the upper edge of it, toes digging into gaps between the bricks, hoisting himself until he found a perch above the grounds, the battlefield laid out in front of him. Ignoring the sick feeling in his stomach, he reclaimed his shotgun and pushed off, to land crouching inside the compound.

Bad move, he thought immediately, but there was no turning back.

One of the posse guards had spotted him already, squealed something incomprehensible, and ran toward Reckford with an automatic weapon clutched against his chest. The Rasta should have fired instead of charging, as he realized too late, when he'd closed the gap by half and saw the new arrival's shotgun pointed at his face.

Recoil stung Reckford's shoulder, but he rode it out and saw his target drop, heels drumming briefly on the turf. He thought about grabbing the dead man's weapon as he passed, then shrugged it off, already laden with more guns than he could use at once. He pumped the shotgun's slide-action, putting another fat shell in the chamber, and moved on.

How would he find the nameless stranger he'd come to locate? And if he couldn't find the man...then, what?

A car theft and a drive for nothing, which would likely get him killed. And if he managed to survive the night, he could look forward to dismissal from the JCF, arrest and trial, maybe a prison term.

The good news: legal problems seemed so trivial right now, they almost made him laugh aloud. Almost.

It came to Reckford that, aside from the stranger he couldn't see yet, everyone else inside the wall was now fair game. It was a posse happy hunting ground, and open season was declared. The best way to survive was to eliminate his opposition, one by one.

Unthinkable, for someone who'd sworn to uphold and defend the law.

But Reckford wasn't working for the law tonight. He had no valid badge and no authority. He *did* know right from wrong, however, and the Viper Posse's dreads had brought this on themselves, through years of preying on the decent people of Jamaica and the outside world.

Scowling as he shot another soldier, and another, Reckford set a course for Quarrie's farmhouse, letting no one stand against him, leaving corpses in his wake.

JEROME QUARRIE REFUSED to panic. It was true that he'd been driven from the last home he possessed, that many of his vehicles had been destroyed and that his soldiers had been dying all around him. Still, he had his wits, his courage and the power of Obeah on his side.

And, of course, the mighty CIA.

He was concerned about Dale Holbrook, wished the

Company had sent a better spy to deal with him. A James Bond type, perhaps, or Jason Bourne. Holbrook was adequate, as far as bagmen went, but he inspired no confidence in combat.

Neither, at the moment, did Usain Dalhouse. The *papaloi* had refused to take a weapon when Quarrie offered him several, simply muttering that the *orishas* would protect him. Which was fine for Dalhouse, but Quarrie still felt better with an AK-47 in his hands. Black magic, in his experience, had never stopped a man as quickly as a bullet did.

"Where are we going?" Holbrook asked, sounding nervous now, if not exactly frightened.

"We're leaving," Quarrie replied, as if that answered everything.

"But leaving *how*?" Holbrook demanded. "Going *where*?"

"Stop asking questions!" he snapped back. "You talk too damn much!"

How was he supposed to know where they were going, how they would escape? Quarrie was making it up as he went along, sorry he'd run to the country at all, when he could have found someplace to hide back in Tivoli Gardens or Trench Town. Now, to have this white man jabbering and nagging at him was intolerable.

Two of Quarrie's soldiers saw him through the battle smoke and ran to join him, both wild-eyed with fear or bloodlust, which looked much the same. One of them blurted out, "Where are we goin, Boss?"

"Never mind," he answered. "Have you seen the white man?"

"No, Boss," the other said.

"Dammit! So why are you standing here?" Quarrie shot back at them.

The soldiers glanced at one another, puzzled, then turned back to Quarrie.

"What should we do?" asked the first one who'd spoken.

"Find the man who killed your brothers. Don't come back without his head."

Another glance between them, then they nodded like a pair of puppets and ran back into the fray. Quarrie supposed he might have sent them to their death, but all he cared about right now was getting off the farm alive, back to the city, where he could conceal himself in some rat hole until the storm had passed.

Holbrook? Forget him, if he couldn't take care of himself. The Company owed Quarrie more than money for the information and assistance he'd provided over time. They should have sent a helicopter for him, with an armed escort to carry him away and stash him somewhere safe.

Dalhouse, the *papaloi*? They were a dime a dozen in Jamaica. He could always find another, better priest to intercede on his behalf with the *orishas*. And if not, that simply meant the gods were overrated, pushing deals they didn't keep.

"We need a car," he told the others, as if that was some astounding revelation.

"Where's mine?" Holbrook asked, peering around the smoky compound.

"You don't remember?"

"Give me a second!"

"We're in a hurry!" Quarrie reminded him. "We'll all be dead soon."

Holbrook snarled a curse, then stopped and pointed. "There, dammit! There it is!"

Bolan found the front door of the farmhouse open. He went inside and started checking its rooms. The lights were out, although the generator was still running, which told Bolan they'd been switched off deliberately. It made searching doubly dangerous, but he got through it and found no one hiding in the house, inside its closets, cupboards, underneath its beds.

He'd missed Quarrie again—but by how long this time?

Despite his sense of urgency, Bolan took time to rig the kitchen. With the Cold Steel blade, he cut the stove's propane line, then sprayed lighter fluid on the range, along the nearby counter tops, and lit it with a match. Time to get out, and he was clear before the gas tank blew, shattering one whole quarter of the house and peeling back its roof, venting hellfire into the night.

It made a satisfying sound and helped light his way besides, but it didn't reveal the man Bolan was searching for. Plain logic told him Quarrie must be somewhere on the grounds, seeking a method of escape, but if he'd bolted for the woods first thing, he would be nigh onto impossible to track.

Don't think that way, he silently told himself.

The posse boss wasn't a woodsman, had probably never spent an hour of his life hiking around a forest. He'd be lost in minutes and would fear that. No. He'd try to flee the same way any other civilized offender would: on wheels.

Which narrowed down the prospects.

Backlit by the house, half of it burning briskly now, Bolan began a counterclockwise sweep of the compound. Passing a pair of off-road motorcycles, he reached down to slash their spark plug wires and leave them useless. The next ride he encountered was a dusty SUV with windows bullet-punctured, but the rest of it intact. He knifed both right-side tires, then drove his Chaos blade into the radiator, through the grille, loosing a gurgling stream of water mixed with coolant.

Three down, and without a bullet wasted to attract attention from the frantic soldiers running every which way, stopping here and there to spray the night with gunfire. Passing corpses of two men he hadn't killed himself, Bolan knew things were starting to unravel for the Viper Posse crew.

He found another car, this one a sporty MG F from Britain, navy blue. He stabbed the front tires, for variety, then popped the hood and cut the wires attached to the engine's distributor cap, turning the car into a pricey paperweight.

SPOTTING THE CAR was one thing. Reaching it, as Holbrook soon discovered, was another thing entirely. Anything could happen with a battle going on, and while it helped to have the Viper Posse's leader at his elbow, neither one of them was bulletproof. The stray rounds flying through the compound were unable to discriminate.

Just ask the witch doctor.

He'd been telling Quarrie something about riding with Holbrook—"Bad luck to travel with a white man"—when the left side of his face erupted, spewing blood and mangled flesh. Holbrook took a second to decipher that he'd been shot from the *right*, a through-and-through that killed him where he stood and dropped him straight down.

Quarrie stood gaping at the body for another second.

"You stupid bastard! Serves you right, you fake. Can't even save yourself? Who are you to tell me anything?" He drove a vicious kick into the dead man's ruined face, then turned to Holbrook, snapping, "Are we going, or not?"

"We're going, absolutely," Holbrook told him, turning from the faceless corpse and picking up his pace. Speed made him a more difficult target, at least in theory.

They reached the car, its diplomatic plates an idiotic joke under the circumstances. Holbrook pressed a button on the key fob and the taillights flashed at him, a loud squawk threatening to draw attention. Up close, he saw that several slugs had struck the vehicle already, one piercing the driver's door, another taking out the window just behind it, yet another through the right-rear window post. The impact dents were bright and shiny, perfect circles where the paint had flaked away on impact.

Holbrook spent a panicked moment circling the car, checking its tires—none flattened yet—and peering at the hood. No damage there, and nothing leaking from below the engine or the radiator. If he quit dicking around and got his ass in gear, they should be good to go.

He cursed the glaring dome light as he slid behind the steering wheel. Quarrie stood waiting for a heartbeat at the other door, as if expecting someone from the sidelines to open it for him, then he did the job himself and settled in the shotgun seat, clutching his short Kalashnikov.

"Come on!" he snapped. "Don't linger here!"

"Who's lingering?" Holbrook replied—and promptly dropped his key somewhere between his feet. "Son of a bitch!"

He missed the dome light now, but wouldn't risk it. Fumbling on the floorboard, cheek against the steering wheel, he thought this was the moment when he'd die, a bullet crashing through his window, piercing his skull, and that would be the end of him.

But no.

He found the key, inserted it, gave it a twist. The small-ish engine came to life immediately. Holbrook was careful not to flood it as he reached down for the parking brake, released it, cranked the gearshift into Drive.

"Hang on," he said, and slammed the pedal down.

WHEN HE'D FIRED the last round from his shotgun, dropping two men with a single cloud of buckshot, Clancy Reck-ford drew his pistol. He dodged toward the nearest build-ing, where he crouched in pitch-black shadow to reload.

The shotgun was a 12-gauge Ithaca 37 pump, capable of slamfiring, wherein a shooter held the trigger down and pumped the slide-action to spray death at his ene-mies in rapid-fire.

A helpful trick at times like this.

He jacked one round into the shotgun's chamber, then slipped seven more into the magazine before he put the Browning Hi-Power away. No one had tracked him to the corner where he'd hunkered down, but he couldn't afford to linger there.

Not if he wanted Jerome Quarrie for himself.

He'd still seen nothing of the stranger who'd led him here, to what might be his final night on Earth. At times, Reckford thought he could track the man's movement by the shifting tide of battle, but he wasn't sure, since some of Quarrie's soldiers seemed to be shooting at each other. High on rum or ganja, maybe panicked by the havoc that surrounded him, they made it easier for Reckford.

Rising to join the battle once again, Reckford won-dered if officers were on the way to break it up. He hadn't called for help and wanted none, even if members of the JCF in Portmore had been willing to respond. He knew a few of them from casual encounters through the years, and most of the instructors at the JCF Academy in nearby

Spanish Town, but couldn't say which ones were on the Viper Posse's payroll. Calling ahead was pointless, anyway, since he'd been suspended and his new civilian status might be in the system, marking him as an outsider undeserving of consideration.

Neva mind, he thought, his brain slipping into the old patois of childhood. He'd come to do this job himself, without backup from the Special Anti-Corruption Task Force. Whatever happened, it was down to him, with or without the American.

And he would see it through alone.

BOLAN WAS ON his fifth vehicle, bending down to knife one of the crew's pickup trucks, when three of Quarrie's soldiers spotted him and rushed at Bolan, howling like berserkers.

Serious mistake.

He left his knife protruding from the off-road tire as it deflated and raised his L85A1. Bolan pegged the nearest soldier and stroked the rifle's trigger once. Piercing the sternum, the round yawed and shattered at the cannelure, exploding through soft tissue in a perfect storm of shrapnel, tearing through the heart, aorta and both lungs.

The guy was dead before he knew it, but he still took two more loping strides, forward momentum overcoming gravity until his brain blanked out and let him drop. Behind him, his companions had no time to reconsider their commitment, as the Executioner shifted his aim.

Next up, the soldier on his left, who had his weapon leveled from the shoulder, rather than the waist, like his surviving cohort. Bolan shot him twice: once in the chest to slow him down, then in the head as he was falling, shattering his skull to fan a crimson halo out behind him, glinting from the firelight as he fell.

The last man up tried stopping in his tracks but couldn't

manage it. His sandals slipped on grass and stole his balance from him, dumping him onto his backside with a squawk of protest. As he hit the turf, his finger jammed the trigger of his Uzi SMG, wasting a burst of Parabellum rounds on empty darkness, somewhere to his left.

He tried correcting it, was halfway there when Bolan shot him through the forehead, one round for the easy kill, and flattened him. The sandals that had tripped him up drummed briefly on the grass, before the last impulses from his gutted brain misfired and slipped away.

Bolan retrieved his knife and sheathed it, looked around for other vehicles to cripple, and had spotted one—a medium sedan—when suddenly its headlights blazed and it began to move. He couldn't see the occupants, much less identify them in the dark, and that meant he couldn't let them get away.

Mental geometry kicked in, and Bolan sprinted off on a collision course.

"WHAT THE HELL'S wrong now?" Quarrie snarled at his driver.

The pale, useless CIA man snapped back at him, void of the proper respect, "We're slipping on wet grass and mud! You couldn't spring for blacktop?"

"Just hurry up!"

"You want to push?"

"I'll push a bullet through your head, you sass me any more," Quarrie replied, jerking the muzzle of his AK-47 in the white man's general direction.

Holbrook muttered something as he grappled with the gearshift, slowly backed the car up several yards, then cranked the steering wheel to drive around the spot where they'd been trapped, long gouges in the lawn. In other circumstances, Quarrie might have flared over the ruined turf, but it meant nothing to him now. His house was gone, the compound was a killing field. It held no memories he wanted to retain.

The only thing he valued now was life itself, and *getting out*.

Holbrook's sedan was gaining traction, swerving slightly as it moved across the broad lawn toward the gates—which, Quarrie saw, were now unmanned. He grimaced, realizing one of them would have to leave the car and clear the path before they could escape. The vehicle was nothing special, far from bulletproof, but it provided more security than open air.

Now, another problem: When they reached the gate, should *he* get out to open it, or leave that job to Holbrook? Could he trust the CIA man not to drive away and leave him in the dust? Conversely, if he told Holbrook to do it— even forced him from the car at gunpoint—what would stop the white man from bolting on foot as soon as he'd cracked the gate enough to slip through it?

Decisions.

As it happened, they never got that far. Some twenty yards from where they'd started, still a long way from the gate and freedom, Quarrie saw a stranger step into the headlights' glare in front of them. He was a black man, not the bastard who'd been wreaking havoc on the Viper Posse during recent days, and not a Rasta, either. He was well armed, with some kind of automatic weapons slung across his back, a shotgun in his hands and aiming at their car's windscreen.

Holbrook blurted out, "Holy shit!" and seemed about to hit the brakes, when Quarrie punched his shoulder.

"Don't stop!" he ordered. "Run him down!"

RECKFORD HAD SEEN the car departing, gambled that the first persons to flee would be Jerome Quarrie and any aids or bodyguards he chose to take along with him. None of the Viper Posse rank and file would dare desert their leader, on pain of agonizing death if he survived the fight and caught up with them later.

Ergo, Reckford had to stop that car, at any cost.

It was a mad dash from his starting point to intercept the nondescript sedan, but he was aided when the car's back wheels lost traction on a wet patch of the lawn. The driver backed it out and drove around the churned-up muck—smart move, bad luck for Reckford—but by then he'd closed the gap enough to have a prayer of catching them.

Shoot now! he thought, but held his fire. Shotguns were tricky, and there'd been no time to swap it with the MP5A3 for greater accuracy. Buckshot started spreading the moment it left a shotgun's muzzle, generally in a cone-shaped pattern. Penetration was another matter altogether: great on wooden doors at point-blank range, less so on speeding cars as they retreated from the gun.

His answer: get in front of the escape car and give it everything he had within a few wild seconds, before leaping to one side. Take out the windshield, driver, front-seat passengers, maybe the radiator and the engine block if that was even possible. Reckford had four live rounds remaining in the Ithaca.

Once he'd stopped the car—or slowed it down, at least—he could ditch the shotgun and bring up the Heckler & Koch SMG. Hit the car and its occupants with thirty Parabellum rounds in less than three seconds, raking the passenger seats. He might have time to reload, if they weren't firing back. Otherwise, pull the Browning Hi-Power and give them his last fourteen shots, counting the one he kept in the chamber.

But first, he had to stop the car. And that, as far as he could see, meant getting out in front of it.

Death wish, Reckford thought, but found an ounce of

extra speed somewhere, lungs straining, heart pounding against his ribs, and leaped into the vehicle's path, stopping short on rubbery legs. Gasping for breath, he aimed the Ithaca, no warning on his lips—he couldn't speak, and had no jurisdiction anyway—as headlights blinded him.

He squeezed the shotgun's trigger, thirty feet and closing, aiming more or less directly at a startled face behind the steering wheel.

White face, he thought, before the car plowed into him and everything turned upside-down.

BOLAN SAW THE CAR strike, heard it *crunch* into the sergeant's body, scooping him up and across its hood. After a jarring impact with the windshield Reckford's buckshot had already perforated, he bounced and rolled across the car's roof, dropping onto the sod behind it.

While the car began to slow and veer off course, losing momentum.

Bolan sprinted after it, dropping a nearly empty STANAG magazine, snapping a fresh one into the receiver on the run. He didn't need to cock his rifle, since it had a live round in the chamber, and the rest would feed from there.

The car had nearly stopped now, and he'd have no problem catching it unless the stunned or wounded driver came around and got his act together in the next few seconds. Far from that, however, Bolan saw the driver's door pop open, dome light flaring, as a front-seat passenger reached over from his side and grappled with the driver's slack form, trying to expel it from the car. He didn't recognize the driver, white beneath a mask of blood, but he saw Quarrie's face under the dome light.

That was all he needed.

Drawing closer, Bolan slowed his pace and kept his

rifle shouldered, covering the vehicle. Quarrie glanced up and noticed him, blinked once and said, "Damn!"

Bolan approached him, walking now, aware of his surroundings and the lack of any other gangsters in proximity. "Ride's over," he told Quarrie.

"Who says so?"

"That would be me."

"And now you're gonna kill me? Why? For who?"

"Who's your worst enemy?" Bolan replied.

"Is that a riddle? How in hell do I know?"

"Check the mirror," Bolan said, and plugged him through the forehead, one round at a range of fifteen feet or less. Quarrie collapsed across the bloodstained driver's seat, facedown, arms dangling from the open door in front of him.

Bolan retreated, kneeling next to Clancy Reckford on the grass. The cop was fading in and out, clearly beyond first aid, his rib cage crushed, his face lopsided from an obvious skull fracture. When his eyes opened, only the left one seemed to focus, locking on to Bolan's face.

"Quarrie?" he gasped.

"All done."

Weak smile, with crimsoned lips and teeth. "He's only part of it, you know."

"I figured."

"Too bad all the others get away."

"Not all of them," Bolan replied. But he was talking to himself.

Epilogue

The day was ending badly, but it could have been much worse. Jerome Quarrie was dead, along with many of his men—the body count still rising as reports came in from Portmore—which was both a problem and, perhaps, a blessing in disguise.

For Perry Campbell, Quarrie's death was problematic because it stopped the flow of Viper Posse bribes to greedy, grasping hands within the JCF and Kingston's government bureaucracy. That was a temporary problem, though. The other posses would expand, absorb the rackets Quarrie had controlled, and they would pay well for the privilege of gobbling up his leftovers.

Conversely, Quarrie's death was providential, since he'd drawn so much adverse publicity in recent days. His survival, if permitted, would have jeopardized the decent men of sterling reputation who allowed him to function on the fringes of society. Without those decent and respected men—himself included—no crime syndicate could function, much less thrive. Of course, the felons were required to pay their dues, in cash and in the other services that made them useful over time.

All things considered, Campbell thought of Quarrie as a blowfly that had buzzed around the feast, alighting here and there to nibble scraps, potentially infecting anything and anyone he touched with the diseases he carried from his roots in Trench Town and Tivoli Gardens. He'd been useful, but he had outlived his usefulness. Now he was gone.

Good riddance.

Campbell thought of Clancy Reckford, frowning for a moment. But again, the news was mostly good. An officer suspended for impeding JCF investigation of a murder spree had cracked, gone on a killing rampage of his own and died as a result. The story could be spun in several ways, all beneficial to the ministry.

Had Reckford been the vigilante killer running wild in Kingston recently?

Was he, in fact, a covert member of the Viper Posse, seeking payback on his boss after his personal corruption was revealed?

Whichever way the story played out in the media, Campbell emerged spotless and smelling like a rose. He was the man who'd removed Reckford from the force, pending investigation and a probable indictment. Reckford's crimes—who knew how many there might be, before the case was closed?—absolved his fellow officers of any taint. He was a lone bad apple in the barrel, the accused who could not speak up in his own defense.

Perfect.

Campbell was finished for the afternoon and ready to go home. He buzzed his secretary, had her call his driver with instructions to be waiting down in the garage. Five minutes. Don't be late. He knew the car would be ready and waiting, bulletproof and air-conditioned for the ride back to his home in Forest Hills.

He cleared his desktop, locked the drawers and left his office, knowing his secretary would be gone within the next few minutes. It was getting late, still light outside, but barely. They had suffered through a hectic day, but all the dirty work—or most of it, at any rate—was done. He feared no repercussions, since a threat to him would also threaten others higher up the food chain, and that could not be allowed.

His car was waiting, as expected, with the sergeant who drove him back and forth to work, to midday meetings, and wherever else Campbell might be required to go during his working hours. Perfectly correct in every move, and wearing a full uniform, his driver held the door for Campbell, then closed it behind him and took his seat up front. They were on their way. Campbell ignored the city scenery he'd seen a thousand times before, much of it squalid and depressing. All so far beneath him that he only gave it thought in terms of personal security.

He traveled with the doors locked, safe within the bulletproof car, behind bulletproof glass. It would take a rocket to kill him in transit, and who cared enough about one bureaucrat to do that?

Arriving at Campbell's home, a large one with a swimming pool in back, his driver stopped the car, walked around and opened the door again. "Tomorrow at the normal time," Campbell remarked, in place of thanks.

"Yes, sir."

The car was off and rolling by the time he reached his doorstep, key in hand, dusk darkening the front porch and its climbing blue dawn flower vines. His key was in the dead bolt before Campbell caught a hint of movement from the corner of his left eye. Turning swiftly, he was startled at the sight of a white man he'd never seen before, aiming a pistol at him, muzzle bulked out by a sound suppressor.

"Perry Campbell?"

"Who are you?" Campbell asked, hating the sudden tremor in his voice.

"What matters is who *you* are."

"What?"

"You're not a cop," the stranger said.

And shot him.

* * * * *

COMING SOON FROM

GOLD EAGLE®

Available July 7, 2015

THE EXECUTIONER® #440
KILLPATH – *Don Pendleton*

After a DEA agent is tortured and killed by a powerful Colombian cartel, Bolan teams up with a former cocaine queen in Cali to obliterate the entire operation.

SUPERBOLAN® #175
NINJA ASSAULT – *Don Pendleton*

Ninjas attack an American casino, and Bolan follows the gangsters behind the crime back to Japan—where he intends to take them out on their home turf.

DEATHLANDS® #123
IRON RAGE – *James Axler*

Ryan and the companions are caught in a battle for survival against crocs, snakes and makeshift ironclads on the great Sippi river.

ROGUE ANGEL™ #55
BENEATH STILL WATERS – *Alex Archer*

Annja uncovers Nazi secrets—and treasure—in the wreckage of a submerged German bomber shot down at the end of WWII.

CNMGE0615